# QUEEN OF MY DOUBLE-WIDE TRAILER

## A SWEET SOUTHERN ROMANTIC COMEDY

### KACI LANE

Copyright © 2023 by Kaci Lane

All rights reserved.

This is a work of fiction. Names, characters, organizations, places, events and incidents are either products of the author's imagination or are used fictitiously. Any resemblance to actual persons, living or dead, or actual events is purely coincidental.

No part of this work may be reproduced, or stored in a retrieval system, or transmitted in any form by any means without written permission from the author.

# QUEEN OF MY DOUBLE-WIDE TRAILER

# CHAPTER ONE

*Liam*

"Oh, I'm not a member." I give Bambi a lopsided grin.

Yes, that's her actual name, or at least the name she goes by in school.

She tilts her head toward the frat house, then at me.

"You said we could go to this party when I asked."

"And we can. Several of my buddies are members."

She crosses her arms. "My big sister said I'm supposed to find a guy from one of our fellow fraternities to take to the mixer."

I shrug. "Okay, go find one."

Her eyes bug.

"What?"

"You just took me out to dinner."

"And?"

She bats her eyes, and her long top lashes catch in her blond bangs. I may as well end this now, since there's no way

I'm paying to sit through her chomping a salad again. Between the nonstop talking and heavy makeup, she reminds me way too much of my Aunt Misty.

"You don't care if I go in that house and look for a new date?" Bambi chokes out.

"Since I don't meet your qualifications, I'd be a fool to hold you back from someone who does."

She pouts until her lips resemble a fish face. I start up the porch to the house, and she catches my arm. "Where are you going?"

"The party."

"Without me?"

I throw up my hands. "Look, you asked to come here, so I brought you. Do you want to go or not?"

Her eyes trail across the front of the house like she's pondering what's inside. I shake my head and brush past her, through the front door.

Kenny Chesney echoes across the room just loud enough for me to make out the lyrics above everyone talking. A mechanical bull is set up where the coffee table usually stays. Three girls in tight skirts attempt to straddle it. One makes it on, then falls off on the first spin. Another falls down laughing at her and spills her White Claw. I let out a long breath and head for the kitchen.

Partying has never been my scene. Maybe I'm an old soul, but I'd rather spend my weekends in a tree stand than doing a keg stand. But I have enough friends here to know where they keep the good stuff.

I reach past a couple making out and open the refrigerator door. In the very back, hidden behind all the alcohol, is a gallon of Milo's sweet tea. I pull it out and smile when I notice the untouched lid.

Nobody's tinkered with it yet, which means it's not spiked.

I find a red Solo cup and pour it full of tea. Then I set the jug on the counter since the kissing couple has plastered themselves in front of the refrigerator. Best not chance accidentally touching the girl and getting myself in trouble.

That's usually how things go for me.

I like to flirt and tease, but I never mess around. I'm all bark and no bite, but somehow that comes back to bite me in the butt.

I chug my tea and head out back to find my friends. If Bambi needs a ride when I'm ready, I'll gladly drop her off. Then I'll never give her a ride—or a date—again.

She's just another name on my long list of disappointing girls. I was told college would have plenty of smart, ambitious women. So far, I've only attracted the type hunting a good time or a Mrs. Degree.

That's not really a thing, though I've overheard plenty of girls say they came to college to find a husband. Good luck with that.

I scratch my head and survey the lawn full of drunken cowboys and semi-preppy country boys. None of them look remotely interested in finding a wife, myself included. Though I admit I wouldn't mind having a girlfriend.

"Liam!"

A thin arm swings around my chest, jerking me back. I steady my cup to keep from spilling my tea before turning around. A tall girl with braided hair smiles and giggles.

I recognize the face, but a name doesn't come to mind.

She attempts to straighten her Christmas headband, but makes it worse. A tiny bell at the top jingles as she fumbles with it.

"I'm wearing mistletoe."

"Actually that's holly. Mistletoe is white."

"Oh, silly." She swipes her hand down my chest.

I take a step to walk away, but she grabs the collar of my

shirt and pulls me to her. She presses her lips to mine before I can shake her loose.

"Liam!"

*How is she yelling and kissing me at the same time?*

I hear my name again and open one eye. Bambi is behind us. I jump back, causing the girl who doesn't know mistletoe to stumble.

"How could you on a date with me!"

"I thought you ended our date."

Bambi's blue eyes turn ice cold. "When did I do that?"

"When you went to look for other guys."

"I never said I was done with you."

"I'm sorry, she just attacked me." I point to holly headband, who isn't amused.

"Attacked you? You kissed me back."

"I . . ." Both girls stare daggers at me as I back away.

My buddy Tiger walks up in a Santa suit. He's holding a black trash bag in one hand. Maybe that's his Santa sack. You never know with Tiger. He swings his arms around the girls' shoulders.

"Ho, ho, ho, who wants to sit on Santa's lap and tell him what y'all want for Christmas?"

Bambi snarls at the trash bag beside her and the braid girl rolls her eyes. They both cut loose and go separate ways.

"Thanks." I smirk at Tiger.

He looks ridiculous drowning in that suit. Not to mention he's wearing a cowboy hat and no beard.

"Must be the suit." He sniffs his sleeve. "Stephen picked it up at a thrift store."

I laugh and drink the rest of my tea.

"What was that catfight about?"

"They're mad at me over nothing, as usual."

He holds his belt and lets out a mock Santa chuckle. I notice he's wearing one of his rodeo belt buckles. Figures. I rarely see him without one. But if I rode bulls, I might be the same way.

"I didn't expect to see you tonight."

"I was on a date with the blond, and she wanted to come here after supper."

He lifts his chin.

"There was a bit of a misunderstanding as to when the date ended."

He nods. "Been there."

Tiger starts walking, picking up trash along the way. I follow him across the backyard and under a volleyball net. He stops at a cooler and grabs two waters, handing one to me.

"Thanks."

We stand at the edge of the property and stare into the road. It's that crazy time of year when everyone is done with finals but nobody has gone home yet.

I stare at Tiger's ridiculous outfit as he chugs his water. His eyes bug and he points toward the road, shaking his hand wildly.

"What?"

He spits some water and gasps. "Ain't that your truck?"

I crane my neck to find my taillights dimming as the truck turns down a side road. "You've got to be kidding me!" I take off running.

Even though I'm running back for my intramural flag football team, steel-toe boots and a belly full of sweet tea don't do me any favors. I whip my arms back and forth to gain momentum. I spot a blond head in the driver's seat right before I catch up to it.

Bambi turns her head, sees me, and gasses it.

I run about another block before she screeches the tires and heads for a different area of campus. I bend with my hands on my knees to catch my breath, then pull out my phone.

"Ho, ho, hello?" Tiger drawls out his words like the crazy cowboy Santa he is.

"Tiger." I pause and catch my breath. "Come get me. I'm halfway to the stadium. I lost the truck when it headed toward town."

"Dude, I've had a margarita."

I sigh. "Just one?"

He hesitates. "You know I'm a lightweight. Anyhow, Conner made it."

Enough said. It was probably ninety percent alcohol and big as a cow trough.

"All right. I'll get an Uber."

I hang up on Tiger and go to the Uber app.

"You've got to be kidding me!" All the Uber drivers are backed up, and based on how everyone looked at the party, Tiger was my best shot at a sober ride.

I scroll through my contacts. Everyone I know here was at the party . . . except.

There's one person I'm certain isn't at a party, because she doesn't go anywhere that's fun. I've never asked her for a favor before, and we're not exactly friends, but she's the most dependable person I know. The ideal choice for when I need someone sober and sane enough to drive me around to find my truck.

I hover over her name for a second before clicking the call button. My ear tingles as the phone rings. I'll likely get a motherly speech about how I shouldn't leave my keys in my truck. If I get my truck, however, it's worth it.

"Hello?"

"Carmelita, it's Liam."

"Liam who?"

*Great.* "Liam Sanderson. You tutor me in chemistry and calculus, and also that one time in history."

"Hey. You had all your finals today, right?"

"Yeah, I need another favor, if you don't mind."

There's a long pause.

"From me?"

I bite my tongue to keep from cursing. For the smartest person I know, she sure is clueless.

"I'm kinda in a time crunch. My truck was stolen and—"

"Have you called the cops?"

I pinch the bridge of my nose. "I know who stole it. I just have to locate it and get it back. You're the only person around I know who's sober right now."

"You're drunk."

I slap my forehead. Why did I call her? "No, I'm sober too, but I need a ride, and there's no Ubers around right now."

I swear, I could've had my cousin three hours away be here by now.

"Where are you?"

My shoulders lift with the hope of getting a ride. I glance around, realizing I've walked farther than I thought while talking to her. "War Eagle Way."

"Stay there, and I'll come get you."

Before I can say thanks, she hangs up. I stare at my phone before returning it to my pocket.

*Should I call the cops?* I don't want to have Bambi arrested or anything. I just want my dang truck back in the condition she found it. I sit on the curb and drop my head in my hands.

A breeze blows through, reminding me it's December. I fold my arms into my chest. Between the mild weather we're having and running like a maniac, I'm just now feeling the chill.

Of course, you wouldn't know it's December with the way most of the girls here are dressed. Except for the one rolling down her window.

Carmelita's head pops out of her tiny red car. She's wearing a thick weather-appropriate sweatshirt.

"Come on."

I hop up and hurry to the passenger side. The inside of her car is super neat and clean, and I'd expect nothing less. She's the type of person you'd expect to one day cure cancer or become president. We met last year in chemistry class. I was fortunate enough to have her as a lab partner.

She was the quiet chick in the back. I sat by her because she was hot. Smart choice on my part, as she's also a genius. It's super rare a girl is both. She's like a unicorn or robot or something.

"Where did it go?"

I'm still so mesmerized at how clean her car is that her voice catches me off guard. "Oh, she headed toward the stadium. I'm afraid she's leaving campus."

"She?" Carmelita raises a brow.

I point toward the road, ignoring the comment. She drives toward the stadium, and we both look out our windows for the truck.

"Was she drunk?"

My stomach buckles. I hadn't considered that possibility. Once inside the frat house, I lost track of her. She seemed sober enough when she tried to fight braided hair, but who knows? Maybe I should've called the cops?

"I'm pretty sure she was sober."

"Pretty sure?" Carmelita raises a brow.

I squirm in my seat. It's like I'm in one of those thriller movies where they pick you up for an innocent ride that turns into an interrogation.

"You should really call the cops."

My hand tingles as I reach for my phone. The last thing I want is to send this gal to jail or put something on her record. I pull out my phone and take my time searching for the campus police number.

Carmelita already knows I'm not that smart, so maybe she thinks nothing suspicious about me taking forever. I'm about to hit the call button when she stops.

I glance out the windshield to find my truck pulled up to the Bo Jackson statue. I drop my phone and jump out. It's still cranked, but I don't see anyone in it.

There's no trace of Bambi or anyone else. Very strange. I double check for anything that might be hers like a purse or something before walking back to Carmelita.

She rolls down the window and squints at my truck. "What happened?"

I shrug. "Beats me. But the truck looks fine. Like she left it here running."

Carmelita frowns. "I'll move back and wait to see if it's drivable."

I nod. "Thanks."

Once she's out of the way, I back up as if everything is normal. I hang my arm out the window and give her a thumbs-up. Then I drive my butt home before anything else crazy can happen.

*Carmelita*

I stand in front of my full-length mirror, holding a blazer in one hand and a blouse in the other. In a few hours, I'll sign all the necessary paperwork for my first full-time job. Even better, it's with the company I've interned for during my undergrad and master's degrees. I settle on the blouse to go with my black skirt in an effort to look professional but not too anxious, then return the blazer to the back of my closet.

A suitcase falls when I reach toward the back. I swallow and push it against the wall. I still haven't made up my mind about Christmas. Papa and Mama want me to go home, as I should. More than anything, I want to spend time with my grandparents. However, I don't want the third degree from everyone about moving back to the island.

They all but kidnapped me when they flew in for my graduation. Now that I'm officially done with school, I have no official excuse for staying here. That is, until I start work full time.

I came halfway across the world to college for a reason, and I'm taking a job here for the same reason. No matter how much I love my family and Filipino traditions, I outgrew Oval Island long ago.

I shrug on the red blouse and button the front, then pull my dark hair over the neck. Sliding into my black heels, I lock up my room and stop in the kitchen for a bottle of water. As soon as I settle into my job, apartment hunting will be a priority. I've spent my entire college career in a shared living space.

My own bedroom and bathroom aren't enough. I want my own kitchen, where I can cook dishes from back home without odd looks.

With my purse in one hand and my water in the other, I head for my car. The parking lot is almost bare, with most students gone home for the holidays by now. I have until the end of the month to move out, which shouldn't be an issue. All of my belongings will fit in two carloads.

I climb in my car and smile at the excitement of a new

apartment. Picking out furniture and new decor is something I've looked forward to for some time. Mama always dictated how I decorated at home, and for the most part, what I wore. One of my favorite things about America is all the freedom of choices. College was my first time making any choices for myself. That scared me at first, but I've grown to prefer it.

Traffic is light, and I make it to the Alabama Science Services building in a few minutes. I'd satisfied my parents with majoring in environmental engineering. They said that would help out the family business greatly. I smiled and said nothing, even though I had no intention of going back home after graduation. Only Lola, my grandmother, knows I've been offered a permanent position here.

I'll eventually tell them all, but not today.

The building is sleek and metal to match the science and computer operations inside. I'll be in the lab, which I prefer. A quiet space to figure things out on my own.

Heat hits me when I open the heavy glass door. My heels click against the tile floor made to look like wooden planks. I greet the receptionist and continue toward Janice's office.

I spot her bright pink dress before anything else. Her earrings are the exact same color, in the shape of flamingos. After I knock softly on her open door, she motions me inside.

"Hi, Mrs. Janice."

"Come in. Have a seat." Her lips press together.

I sit in front of her desk, expecting her to slide me a stack of papers. Instead, she sits in her chair and sighs.

"I'm afraid I've got some unfortunate news."

My eyebrows raise so high I get a headache.

Janice clicks her computer mouse and stares at the screen.

"What's wrong?" I ask hesitantly.

She turns to me. "Your visa is expired."

"It's still good."

She wavers her head. "If you were a student, but you graduated last week."

"So what can I do to extend it?"

Janice clicks something on her computer and scrolls her mouse. "Have you applied for OPT?"

My palms start to sweat. Since I haven't heard of the term, I'm guessing that's a no.

She glances at me and must read my mind. "Optional Practical Training."

"Oh no, ma'am. But I have a STEM degree and, as you know, have interned here the past two years."

She frowns. "Sorry, hon, I'm afraid that's not enough. You have to file certain paperwork to get approval for the extension."

I let out a large breath and steady myself before responding. *Do not freak out.*

"Can I do that now, like today?"

"You can start the process, but even once the ball is rolling, there's no guarantee you'd get approved."

"No guarantee?" My voice squeaks.

"You have to prove that you're so valuable to the company that they will grant it. That's why you should've started the process months ago."

"Why didn't you tell me?" I swallow, on the brink of crying.

"Carmelita, I'm so sorry, but it wasn't my responsibility. I had no idea what you had set up until this morning when I pulled your paperwork. These are questions you should've gone over with an advisor or maybe a professor."

I breathe in and out, my chest shaking. This is the problem with everyone always arranging things for me. My culture has prepared me to succeed in many ways, but not when it comes to making decisions.

Between my parents, my grandparents, and our housekeeper, I never even had to think about food. When the clock hit a certain hour, snacks would magically appear. My first time in the student food court was like sifting through hits on Google search.

"Any advice on how to prove I'm valuable?"

Janice shrugs. "We can put in a good word about your work here, and you have excellent grades from school. However, there are tons of applicants for this position, many with advanced degrees and more work experience than you."

I stare at my hands, which are fisted around the ends of my pencil skirt. I relax my fingers and run them across the wrinkles I made on my clothing.

"If you plan on staying in the States long-term, you're better off to apply for a green card. You can apply as working in the sciences."

"And that will work?"

Janice laughs. "Maybe, but you'd have better luck if you were married."

"Pardon?"

"If you were married to a US citizen, then it would be another reason to get the process moving. And though it may take a while, they're certain to approve it."

Once I realize Janice isn't joking, I unhinge my jaw enough to respond. "So you're suggesting I get married?"

She taps her fingernails on the desk and gives me a complacent stare. "I'm not suggesting anything, simply giving you all the options."

I nod.

She types something else on the keyboard and turns her screen to me. "I can email you this information about how to apply and—"

My phone buzzes in my purse. I silence it. "Sorry about that."

"I'll email you all the links. Everything can be done

online now. In the meantime, I'll notify Rodney about your status."

"What do I do now?" I wipe my hands across my skirt again.

I'd planned on starting work today, or at the latest tomorrow.

"Keep me posted. I'll try and hold the position open as long as I can, but there's a lot of great applicants."

I bite my bottom lip and nod. "Thanks for all your help."

"Sure thing, hon. Take care."

I force a slight smile and let myself out. Janice gives me a sympathetic face. I'd bet my bank account she's silently blessing my heart, like all the women her age do around here in these situations.

Except my situation is a little trickier than most.

My phone buzzes again. I answer without checking the caller. "Hello?"

"Darling, how's your day going?"

I open my car door and fall into the seat. The last person I want to talk with right now is my mother.

"Good," I lie. "How's everything there?" I almost said "home," but stopped myself in time.

"We miss you."

I laugh. "You saw me last week."

"I know, but we're ready for you to come home anytime. The island is decorated beautifully. You've already missed most of the holiday."

I rest my forehead against the steering wheel. While Americans start advertising and marketing Christmas in the fall, we start celebrating Christmas in the fall. I always argued it's not as special that way, but Mama loves the opportunity to dress up our property and host events.

"I'm actually pretty busy right now," I lie again.

Guilt washes through me. I don't usually lie to Mama,

especially twice in one conversation. I prefer to omit information instead. Like the fact that I'm about to start a job at Auburn as soon as I can get my citizenship situation settled.

A country song plays loudly beside me. I close the car door, thinking it's someone driving nearby. Then the main part of the chorus repeats itself two more times.

"Mama, I've got to go. I'll call you back. Love you!"

I commit the ultimate sin by hanging up on her. Then I reach across the passenger seat and fumble around the floorboard until I spot a phone lighting up.

The caller ID says "Tiger" across the screen. I pick up the phone and notice the background is Liam holding a buck. *Liam's phone.* He must've dropped it last night.

I dismiss the call, since I'm in no mood to explain to whomever Tiger is why I'm on the other end of the line. It might be the girl who stole his truck. Sounds like a stripper name, but that's none of my business.

However, I do need to return this phone. And since I won't be working today, I have time to now.

# CHAPTER TWO

*Carmelita*

I don't generally make house calls, but I have gone to Liam's trailer twice. I've tutored him more than most clients, since several of our classes overlapped and he needed help in most.

I wouldn't call Liam dumb at all, more like uninterested. He's the type who would do great out in the work field, but doesn't do well in the classroom with tests and textbooks. Whenever we did hands-on assignments, he often outperformed me. Too bad most of our grades relied on written tests.

Tiger Fields isn't far from campus, nor from Alabama Science Services. He lives alone on the back street with most of the other older mobile homes. Had I not already known him well, there's no way I'd go someplace like this alone at night to tutor a guy.

But it's Liam.

I've never heard him curse or seen him drink alcohol. He

owns a lot of guns, but all hunting rifles. In fact, that's about all he does is hunt. For the most part, he's harmless. Both times I came here before, he offered me sweet tea when I arrived, then stood on the porch and watched until I drove away safely.

Actually, he's more than harmless. He's a gentleman with a strong streak of redneck flair.

The only difference in Liam and the upper-class guys back home is that they don't say "y'all" or put ice in their tea.

I park beside his truck, which appears to have made it back unscathed. Three concrete blocks lead to his front door. An envelope with his name printed on the front is taped to the storm door. I ignore it and knock since there isn't a doorbell.

After a minute in the cool air with no answer, I knock louder. A few seconds pass, then I hear footsteps from the back. The vinyl door pops open to Liam in a pair of boxer briefs.

I shield my eyes and lean back. My heel catches on the edge of the step and I start to go down. A hand wraps around my waist and pulls me inside.

The door slams shut, and I wince. With my hand still covering my eyes, I try and erase what I just witnessed. Liam, in his underwear, with ruffled hair.

"You can look now."

I blink open one eye and peek through my fingers to find him wearing a camouflage-print throw blanket around his waist.

"Sorry about that. Most anyone here this early has already seen me like this."

"No comment." I exhale and drop my hand, then raise my other hand that's holding his phone. "I found this in my car."

"Oh thanks." He yawns.

"Sorry I didn't notice last night."

"It's all right. I haven't missed it. I just woke up."

I blink. "It's close to ten by now."

"So?"

I shake my head. "Anyway, I'll get out of your hair." I reach for the door.

Liam snakes his arm around and pulls it open for me, then rips the envelope. "What's this?"

I shrug and continue down the steps to my car.

"You've got to be kidding me!"

I jerk my head back to him poised in the doorway, the throw still around his waist. I continue walking and reach for my car door, then stop. Whether it's empathy or nosiness, I turn and go back toward Liam.

"What's wrong?"

He shoves the paper toward me and runs a hand over his hair.

I scan the document, which looks official. It's from the mobile home park and states that he has until January 1 to upgrade his trailer.

"Why would they do this? My trailer has been here since nineteen eighty-six." Liam slaps the door frame and a piece of vinyl chips off.

It falls beside my shoe in the grass. I bend to pick it up, then rub my arms at the chill when I stand quickly.

"I'm sorry. Where are my manners? Take my blanket."

"Liam, I—"

Before I can finish saying I don't need it, he tosses the blanket at my face. I drop my gaze to the ground as I wrap it around my shoulders.

"Be right back," I hear him call as the door slams again.

I glance around the park and nod at an older man in the lot beside Liam's. He tips his cap and continues working on his truck.

Liam returns in jeans and a long-sleeved T-shirt. He narrows his eyes at me. "I've never seen you so dressed up."

"I thought I was starting my new job today."

He laughs. "At that place called—"

"Don't say it!"

"Okay, but you know I'm not the only one who's noticed."

I roll my eyes. Although I'd never admit it, one of the first things I noticed about Alabama Science Services was the company's initials. My first semester interning, a marketing intern was let go for making a letterhead with the acronym and printing it on a large quantity of envelopes. A longtime client called a week later to say he got a company Christmas card from "a rather colorful return address."

Liam smiles, and I momentarily forget that I'm about to be deported and he's about to be homeless. The man next door bangs something against his truck, jolting me back to reality.

"Anyway, I didn't start my work visa process soon enough to start my job."

Liam scratches his head. "I thought you had like a green card or something?"

I chuckle. "I wish."

"Why don't you just get one of those, then?"

"It's not that simple. Trust me, I asked."

He crosses his arms and sighs. "Well, you helped me last night. If there's any way I can help you with that, let me know."

"You can marry me," I say sarcastically.

He bursts out laughing so hard that I'm a bit offended. "Is it that absurd to think someone would marry me?"

He coughs. "No, just funny that you thought I should."

"What's wrong with that?"

He balks. "We're polar opposites."

"Yeah, but what's wrong with marrying me?"

"Nothing, for someone else."

My jaw drops. Is he insinuating I'm not good enough for him?

"What does that mean?"

"I dunno. Nothing against you. I don't date smart girls, is all."

"Clearly, since your last date stole your car."

"Now that's just wrong." He narrows his blue eyes at me.

I stare at the ground, regretting my last comment, but not enough to apologize just yet.

"If it makes you feel any better, I'm about to lose my residence."

I look up. "Sorry about that. At least you'll still have the lot, right?"

He laughs. "A lot of good that'll do. If they won't let me have an old trailer, I doubt they'll let me pitch a tent."

"At least you don't have to find a place to live and a husband."

"Darling, if I ever go looking for a husband, something's terribly wrong."

My stomach twitches. Nobody's ever called me "darling" before, and there's something soothing in the way Liam drawls out the word to about four syllables. He smiles wider, and my stomach twists harder. Most likely it's from stress piled onto nothing but water all day. However, I don't care to hang around and find out.

"I'll let you get back to sleep or whatever you have planned for the day." I step toward my car and open the door.

Stupid blanket. I unwrap my shoulders. When I turn to take it back, I bump into Liam's chest. I raise the throw in my fisted hands.

"You can keep it if you need it," he says.

"I may not have a job yet, or a home for long, but I do have blankets."

He smirks. "I would offer you my extra bedroom, but it's about to get demolished."

My cheeks flush when he mentions a bedroom. Even though it's an extra bedroom, Liam mentioning it catches me off guard.

"Good luck with that." I give him an awkward thumbs-up and slide into my car.

He backs up so I can close the door. Then I drive away, trying to ignore the neighbor peeing beside his truck and Liam wearing a smirk that flips my stomach even more.

*Liam*

Did Carmelita just ask me to marry her?

Clearly, she was being sarcastic. But as I stand in the yard and watch her drive out of the trailer park, my mind conjures up images of her in a long white dress with a ring on her finger.

I shake my head to snap myself out of it. The last thing I need in my life is a woman, especially one I'd have to keep up.

What a proposal that would be. *Hey, you think I'm kinda stupid and my house is getting destroyed, but want to get married?*

If last night wasn't a sign I need to stay single, this is.

I shake my head at Tom taking a whiz by his truck. He

thinks he's being discreet, but dropping his jeans to his knees gives it away.

I ball up the blanket in my hand and go inside. Good thing about Carmelita waking me up is I can get a head start on finding a new place.

The linoleum floor squeaks when I hurry across the kitchen for my laptop. This place could fall apart any day, but it's *my* place. I chose this trailer my freshman year. It's on a quiet street and fits my nonchalant attitude. If I'd gotten a new mobile home, then Mama would be on me to clean up and "keep it nice."

When she visits me here, she blesses my heart and brings me lots of homemade candy.

I plop down in my recliner, which is fairly new. Call me an old man if you will, but a comfy place to sit is a priority. I recline slightly and pop out the legs before opening my laptop.

Living in an apartment sounded confining when I came to college. But I doubt Daddy would buy me a new trailer for one more year here, so I need to find something for the cost of my current bills.

My eyes bug when I click on a few search results from googling "apartments near Auburn campus." Rent alone is more than my bills and lot rent for this place. None of them include utilities, which would make this even more expensive.

As much as I enjoy my privacy, I'll have to get a roommate.

Might as well live with someone I like.

Carmelita pops in my head, but I quickly deflate that idea. Getting an apartment with her might be an easy solution, but not a smart one. No way I could live down the hall from a hot girl for too long and not flirt.

That's it. I'm going to my boys. I slam the laptop and pop

the legs down on my recliner. Surely someone in the frat house will want an apartment with me.

I make a mental checklist of all the guys I could stand to share a space with on a daily basis. There's two, maybe three, with Tiger topping the list.

By the time I'm at the house, I have a monologue prepared to convince him to move out. I hurry up the porch steps and open the door. A chicken peeps at me before bobbling out the door. I shake my head and continue inside.

Marshall glares at me from the living room.

"Hey, man. Is Tiger around?"

He points toward the hall, then stares out the window.

"Thanks." I wave a hand and head for the hallway.

Tiger is at his desk when I reach his room. I don't see Conner anywhere in the small room. Great, I can talk Tiger into leaving that idiot and rooming with me.

"Tiger."

He leans back in his desk chair and smirks. "What brings you here in the daylight?"

Valid question since I'm not in the frat. Most of my visits are when there's some event or they have a card night and want more players.

"I have a proposition for you."

"Oh snap. I was worried something happened when you didn't answer your phone earlier."

"It was—" I catch myself before mentioning Carmelita. "I was probably still asleep." That's a true statement.

"What's up?"

I pull the trailer park letter from my back pocket and unfold it. Tiger takes it from my hand and reads it.

"Dude!"

I nod and take back the paper. "I know, right?"

"Sit." He points to his bottom bunk and spins his chair to face it.

I sit on the edge of the unmade bed and rest my elbows on my knees.

"What are you gonna do?"

Daddy always told me that people have a hard time saying "no" when you look them in the eye. I give Tiger my most sincere, pitiful—yet stern—stare.

"I was thinking you and me get an apartment."

"No."

My eyebrows shoot up. Not the answer I expected from my best bud. Especially after I glared at him like a hurt hawk. "What do you mean *no*?"

"I mean no, as in the opposite of yes."

I sigh.

"It's not you, bro. I have to stay here. I'm paid up through the school year and hopefully graduate in May. It would make no sense for me to get an apartment. After I graduate, that would be sweet, but not now."

I nod. "I get it."

"Marshall may need a place next semester."

I wince. "Pass."

"He's quiet."

"Yeah, too quiet. He creeps me out. Besides, I once saw him pick his nose while talking to a girl."

Tiger laughs. "Dude, what are we, junior high now?"

"Exactly. He shouldn't be picking his nose around girls."

Tiger drops his head in his hands. "I could let you crash here a night or two, but after too long, they'll kick you out or make you pledge."

"I understand." I stand, careful not to bump my head on Conner's top bunk. "Text me if you hear of anything?"

"Yeah, bro." Tiger snaps his fingers. "Have you checked those boards around campus where they post like lost dogs and stuff for sale?"

"No, why?"

"Sometimes they have rooms for rent there too."

"Thanks, man." I extend my hand.

Tiger grabs it and gives it one big pump before letting loose. I leave him to whatever it is he does when I'm not around.

Stephen passes me in the hallway, followed by a couple of underclassmen carrying boxes. I greet them and hurry toward the exit.

Marshall is still alone in the living room. Now he's staring at the ceiling fan like a baby. I shake my head and get out of this joint.

I take photos of all the "Roommate Wanted" flyers on the message board. There aren't a lot, but enough worth calling about. Somehow I prefer taking my chances with a total stranger over living with someone I know but don't like—specifically Marshall.

On the off chance I can go look at a place, I sit in my truck to make the calls. The first person to answer is a woman. Already a red flag for obvious reasons. When she tells me she's twenty-five with two kids and wants to rent out the spare bedroom to pay daycare fees, I politely decline.

Next I call a number that says it's out of order. I try texting it too, but get the same result. Scratch that. On to my last lead.

I recognize the name of the apartments. It's a nice complex not too far from where I live now. It even has a pool. I call the number and perk up when a normal-sounding dude answers.

"Yeah, you can come by now. I'm on my lunch break."

"Okay. I'll be right by."

I shove my phone in my pocket and sigh with relief. How awesome would it be to have something lined up today?

I drive to the complex and find the unit. It's on the top floor, far enough from the pool to not cause a ruckus when I'm trying to sleep. This is looking better and better.

After two knocks, a guy answers the door. He's wearing a *Mario Kart* T-shirt and has a beard but no mustache. His glasses are small circle frames like old dudes wore in history books.

"I'm Liam. I called about the room."

"Bernard." He smiles. "Where are my manners? Come in."

He opens the door wider, and I walk into the strangest sight. Considering I grew up in Wisteria, Alabama, that's saying something.

My mouth drops as long rat-squirrel-like creatures mingle around the room like pet cats.

"Uh, are those—"

"Yep, ferrets." Bernard picks one up and nuzzles it under his chin.

I shift uncomfortably as he talks to it like my grandma does babies. Human babies.

"I foster them and keep around a dozen at a time."

"A dozen?" The shock comes through in my tone.

"Yeah, I had fifteen once, but the health department gave me a slap on the wrist for that." He snorts.

I shove my hands in my pockets in case he asks me to hold one.

"One reason the room is so cheap is because part of your duties as my roommate will be cleaning their cages."

*Oh, heck no!*

"I mostly work nights, but I put in overtime sometimes."

"What do you do?"

"I run a comic store."

I lift my chin. That doesn't seem too strange, especially for a guy with an Amish beard in a gamer shirt who fosters ferrets.

"There's an adult video rental in the back." He winks.

My skin crawls. I've seen and heard enough. Too much, actually.

"So, what do you say, Liam?"

"I don't think this will be a good fit for me."

Bernard's eyes go hooded, and I'm afraid I've offended him. He hugs the ferret tighter.

I back up a few feet toward the door. Bernard follows. He's starting to scare me. I grew up playing football and have a gun in my truck. But he's a bigger dude and this is his home turf. And he's got like an army of ferrets running around. If they're trained, I'm a dead man walking.

Like a sign from heaven, I spot a glass Coke bottle on a shelf. The sun hits it just right, highlighting The University of Alabama logo on the front.

"Dude, I can't live with a Bama fan. I'm an Auburn student."

"Huh?"

I nod toward the shelf. Soon as he turns his head, I dart out the door and make a beeline for my truck. Then I haul butt out of the parking lot and head for my trailer.

My heart pounds as I open my own front door. I lock it behind me and slide to the floor. The shag carpet engulfs me like a warm towel. Why can't I keep this place? It's scary out there. I don't like it.

I lie back and ignore the rotting floor underneath me. This place could last another year. That's all I need. One year, and I'll be done with classes. I'll be co-oping full-time and can afford something better. Hopefully somewhere closer to Wisteria, maybe Tuscaloosa.

I roll onto my side, and my body dips with the creaking floor. What was I thinking? This trailer should've been condemned a long time ago. It's old enough to be my parent, or arguably my grandma. I sigh and pull out my phone to text. There's only one option left.

**Hey, it's Liam. Can you meet me for Mexican later?**

Three dots appear, causing my heart rate to increase. I can't believe I just texted her. There's no turning back now.

**What do you need?**

I swallow the lump in my throat.

**I want to get to know you better before I agree to marry you.**

# CHAPTER THREE

*Carmelita*

I've officially gone mad.

Instead of driving home for a relaxing day after work, I'm driving to a Mexican restaurant to discuss a possible marriage proposition. How did my life flip on edge in one day?

If only I'd applied for that stupid work visa sooner. Why didn't I ask someone for guidance? I've been so darn used to people laying out every step for me from birth that I naively assumed someone would've told me what to do without asking.

Well, I'm an adult now and the damage is done. That leaves me with two options. I can run home to my parents and live the life they have planned for me on Oval Island. One that involves the family business and eventually marrying Mr. Oval Island Heir himself—Antonio Ramos. Both our families would love nothing more than to officially merge.

Antonio has had eyes on me since we were kids. His ancestors settled our tiny island and have run it ever since. Last I heard, he's in law school, being groomed to take over one day. Marrying him would be like a modern-day fairy tale for him and our extended families. For pretty much everyone on the island . . . except me.

Despite his dashing K-Drama good looks, rich pedigree, and charming personality, I'm not in love with him. And believe me, I've tried to love him as more than a friend on several occasions. That spark isn't there for me, which leads me to option two.

Marry a redneck from a nice family in Alabama, start my job, and lie low until my green card is approved. Then I can get an annulment and live happily ever after.

Ugh. That's not a good fairy tale either.

So what if I'm not meant to have a fairy-tale marriage? I can at least have a fake marriage and land my dream career. Right?

I pull up to the restaurant and park. From my car, I watch Liam through the window. He's at a table eating chips and salsa. My stomach turns as I reach for the door handle.

I can do this. There's nothing wrong with Liam. He's a little skinny, but handsome. He's also a good man. A little goofy and immature, but aren't most Americans our age?

*You can do this. It's the easiest option.*

I jerk open the car door and hurry inside the restaurant. A waiter greets me right before Liam spots me. He lifts his arm and smiles.

I turn to the waiter. "I found the guy I'm meeting." He nods as I pass.

"What's up?" Liam greets me around a mouthful of chips.

I force a tight-lipped smile and slide into the booth across from him.

He swallows and wipes his hands together. "For a minute I thought you weren't going to show."

"I almost didn't," I admit.

"I almost didn't text," he admits.

"Are we crazy?" I rest my elbows on the table and sigh.

"More desperate, I'd say."

"Can I get you started with some drinks?" The same waiter appears at our table.

"Sweet tea," we say in unison.

"Jinx." Liam points to me and winks.

A slight flutter hits my stomach. I blame it on eating nothing more than a bag of pretzels all day, but I realize it happened right after he winked. I stare at the wooden table in front of me.

"You're unjinxed so we can talk," he mumbles around more chips. Then he points to the basket between us. "Help yourself."

I reach for a chip, my hand shaking. This is awkward. How do you start a conversation with the guy with whom you're contemplating fake marriage? I don't. I let him start it.

"Here's what I'm thinking. We both need a place to live. Since I have the lot, it makes more sense to purchase a new mobile home. That will give us more space and some assets to split when we . . ." Liam breaks a chip in half and drops the two pieces on the table.

I nod. "Can you find a new one that soon?"

He smirks. "Yes. As a matter of fact, I know from my aunt's ex that there's a mobile home festival not too far from here every December."

"Really?" Add that to the long list of things that amaze me about Alabama.

"Yeah. Only problem is I don't have a ton of cash flow right now. I didn't budget for something like this, and might've spent most of my reserve on a new deer cam."

"Might've?"

"Okay, so I did." He picks one of the broken chips off the table and pops it in his mouth. "But I start back co-oping part-time in January. I could also bring some corn from back home and sell it to hunters as a side gig. Maybe you could pick up some more clients at night."

"Your drinks." The waiter slides a glass in front of each of us. "Are you ready to order?"

Liam raises his brows at me.

"Go ahead," I tell him, then open my menu for the first time.

I scan the dinner menu as he orders something called an Eagle Burrito. Anyplace other than Auburn, I might worry it was stuffed with eagle meat.

"Shrimp tacos. Thank you." The waiter gathers our menus and leaves. "I can help cover the costs easily," I tell Liam.

He perks up. "You sure? I don't want to overwork you or anything."

I laugh. "It's fine."

I don't advertise that my family owns a very successful pearl and gemstone business. Thanks to my frugal living style, I have plenty saved in my college account. I'd planned on using it for a down payment on a house after I meet and marry someone. Given the circumstances, I might as well use it for a mobile home after I marry a decent guy I somewhat know.

So much for living that American dream.

"I'm serious. You don't have to meet with clients all night if that's too much after your day job."

"It's fine, I promise."

We sit in silence for a few minutes as he munches on chips and studies my face. Either he thinks I'm lying about having the money or about giving it for this. I put on a

## QUEEN OF MY DOUBLE-WIDE TRAILER

sincere face to try and prove I'm not full of crap. After examining me fully, he finally speaks.

"So you're good with putting up most of the money for it? I'll pay you back over time, and you can get back everything you spend and more once . . ."

He holds up a chip with both hands. I place my hand on his before he breaks it this time.

"I get it, Liam, you don't have to keep wasting chips."

He moves his hands away from mine and pops the chip in his mouth.

"I was gonna eat it regardless," he says as he chews.

I laugh, and he smiles. I realize I'm still holding my hand where it was on his and jerk it back. I've had more physical contact with him in the past twelve hours than I have the entire time we've known one another.

"Yes, I can buy the trailer."

A plate bangs against the table, jerking me to attention. The waiter shoves it toward Liam, then slides my tacos toward me. He gives me a concerned stare.

"Is everything okay?"

"Can we get some extra napkins?" Liam asks.

The waiter stares at me for an answer.

"Yes, thanks."

He walks away, but keeps his eyes on me for a bit. Strange.

I shake it off and pick up a taco.

I grab a pen from my purse and unfold my napkin. "We need an official agreement."

Liam licks some salsa dripping down his hand. "Isn't that what a marriage license is?"

"Yes, but I'm meaning more like ground rules."

"Oh, like 'no leaving the toilet seat up' stuff. Don't worry I grew up with a sister."

I swallow a bite of my taco and try and ignore the toilet

comment. Then I make a mental note to get a place with two bathrooms.

"At most, the green card should take a year, which is around the time you graduate, correct?"

"Yep."

"Perfect. We can plan an annulment for then." I jot down "one year" on the napkin.

"You mean divorce."

I look up from the table.

"Neither of us is crazy or criminals or cousins, so the state ain't gonna grant an annulment."

I squint. "How is it you know about the annulment laws in Alabama, but needed my help counting the gate money for a rodeo?"

He crosses his arms. "I did my research before coming here."

I take a long drink of my tea, then press my lips together. I take a minute to study Liam. Beneath his barbarian eating habits and nonchalant persona, there's a lot of common sense. He doesn't think like your average guy with a closet full of camouflage—and that's a good thing.

"Oddly enough, I feel better about this arrangement now."

"Let me ask you something." He cocks a grin.

I nod for him to go ahead as I chew on a taco.

"Why me?"

The waiter returns with a stack of napkins. "Sorry about the wait. More tea?"

"Yes, please," I say.

He refills my glass as Liam slides his to the edge for a refill too.

"Of course, it started as a joke. Then I realized how badly I need help. I don't get out much. All I really know are the people at work, my dorm, and my clients. Everyone at work is old or odd." I snarl my nose.

"Why not another client?"

"You're the only one I've met off campus, and most of them are women."

Liam stands as tea trickles down the table onto his lap.

"Sorry about that." The waiter stops pouring the tea and shoves the extra napkins toward him.

He dabs the small wet spot on his leg, then frowns at his seat.

I slide toward the wall and move his plate beside mine. "Here, sit by me."

He comes to my side of the booth, which isn't that wide. Our thighs brush as we settle in our seats.

"Thanks." He smiles at me. "That waiter was checked out."

I glance at the napkin where I wrote "one year." My fingers shake as I push it toward Liam. This is it. I'm proposing a marriage of convenience over soft tacos.

*Don't back out. Your only alternative is shucking oysters with Antonio.*

Liam reaches for the napkin, and our fingers brush. My hand stops shaking, as if him taking the note subconsciously calms me.

I hold the pen between us. He stares at it a beat before taking it. I watch as he scribbles his first and last name beneath my writing.

He holds the pen toward me. "Your turn."

"Miss!"

I jerk my gaze to the edge of our table, where the waiter stands with a mop. He shakes his hands wildly. "Please, whatever kind of business he's got you in, don't sign."

I wrinkle my brow. "Excuse me?"

"You don't need his clients. Please, I can get you a hostess job here so you won't need this pimp."

The waiter's face shows genuine concern. I turn to Liam, whose face is full of confusion, then I burst out laughing. He's still confused when I answer the waiter.

"Sir, this isn't what you think, but I appreciate your concern. Can you please bring me a to-go box?"

He nods, but frowns and hurries away.

"And the check!" Liam calls after him before smiling at me.

I scribble my signature beneath his before I chicken out. Our first and last names blur together as I concentrate on the napkin. Might as well get used to seeing this.

Soon we'll sign a marriage license.

*Liam*

"Want some brownies? My mama made them over the weekend."

Carmelita raises the corners of her mouth. "I'll take one."

I set a brownie on a paper towel for her and grab two for me. Then I open the fridge and grab the milk. One quick sniff changes my mind. I pour it down the sink and get us two bottles of water.

I toss the empty jug in the corner trash can, basketball style. "Score."

Carmelita frowns.

"What?"

She doesn't say anything, but wets some paper towels and

wipes the stream of milk that dots my kitchen floor. She neatly pushes the paper towels into the trash, then rejoins me at the counter. Getting married to her might not be so bad.

"Let's go in here. The stools aren't so reliable."

She follows me to the living room and sits on the couch across from my recliner. "Why don't you get rid of the stools?"

I chuckle. "I guess it will all be gone soon enough."

"We may need a storage unit to store anything you plan on keeping before the new home moves in."

"Good point, and your stuff too."

"Most of mine will fit in my car."

"Really?" I ask around a mouthful of brownie.

"The dorms were furnished."

Her eyes scan the room from one wall to the next, studying my mounted deer heads and football posters. When her gaze makes it back to me, she takes a tiny bite of the brownie.

"Oh wow. This is so good," she says after she swallows.

"Yeah. Mama's a great cook. So is my aunt. She even has a baking show coming."

"That's so cool."

I nod and finish one of my brownies in a huge bite. We both nibble in silence for a second. After the waiter weirded out, I suggested we come back here to talk about the arrangement. In hindsight, it might've sounded suggestive, but Carmelita drove herself on her own free will. Besides, she wouldn't agree to marry me if she were scared of me.

"When were you thinking of doing a wedding?" I ask.

"Tomorrow."

I choke on my water.

"Are you okay?" She stares at me as I beat my chest to try and dislodge the water.

I cough like a clogged drain, then clear my throat and

nod. "Maybe it's different where you grew up, but when my sister got married, it was a big deal. Mama and her planned stuff for like a year and had this big deal at my uncle's house."

She laughs. "Not necessary. We can go to the courthouse."

My eyes widen. I'm half relieved that we don't have to make a big deal of it, but half sad that Carmelita won't get a dream wedding. Girls live for that sort of thing.

"We only need to sell this wedding to my employer and anyone checking for the green card. No need to tell our families."

I lift my chin. If she's ashamed of marrying me, then I take back the sad. Now I'm half mad. I chew on my second brownie and mull over what she said. My family not knowing could be a good thing.

I nod. "Good idea. My family can get a little nosy."

"My family invented nosiness."

"Darling, wait until you've been to Wisteria."

Her cheeks redden. She stays quiet, so I continue.

"If we're able to keep this marriage a secret, then you'll never have to go there."

A slight smile comes across her face. She sips her water and relaxes against the back of the couch for the first time. A few seconds of silence pass.

"Liam, I really appreciate you doing this."

"Hey, you're the one buying me a new home."

She laughs nervously. "That's just money. Marrying someone is a big deal."

"Agreed. And I wouldn't marry just anyone."

"That's good to know." She smiles.

We share a laugh, then her face goes serious. "Before we go through with this, I want to make sure you're totally okay with it."

I lean forward. "Well, yeah." I pull the napkin from my front shirt pocket. "I wouldn't have signed this if I wasn't."

She bites the corner of her lip.

"I'm serious," I reassure her.

Carmelita's lips quiver, then her shoulders shake. A tear drips down her cheek. I set my water on the end table and join her on the couch. "What's wrong?"

She shakes her head. "This isn't how I pictured getting married."

"If it makes you feel better, neither did I."

She sniffles and more tears fall. I scoot an inch closer and rest my hand on her upper back. She falls against my chest and cries more.

My nerves jerk around like an electric fence. Her tears soak my shirt, and I tighten my grip around her back. "Carmelita," I whisper. "You don't have to do this. I don't want to be the guy who ruins your life."

She sniffles and lifts her head. It's within a few inches of mine. I swallow.

"You're not ruining my life. It was my idea. I asked you for a reason."

I drop my arm from around her and collapse against the back of the couch. She jerks her head toward me. "*Not* marrying you would ruin my life."

"What do you mean?"

She stares at her lap and picks at her nails. I wait for her response, not wanting to push.

"I can't go home."

I wrinkle my forehead. Is her island not safe? If that's the case, she needs more than me to set things right.

"My parents have this whole life planned for me, but it's not what I want."

She lifts her eyes to me and frowns. I give her what I hope is a kind face to let her know she can talk about it.

"It's always been assumed I would live on the island, work in the family industry, and marry the governor's son, who will one day be in charge."

I lift my finger in thought, but can't put the question into words.

"Our island is tiny. One family founded it long ago. That family has governed the island ever since. My family has been there since the beginning as well. It's always been assumed we would marry."

"Why?"

She shrugs and wipes at her eyes.

"And in America, you can work where you want and marry who you want."

She nods and sniffles.

"But you want to fake marry me?"

"It sounds crazy, I get it. But, Liam, I trust you, and we can help each other out."

I puff up my cheeks and fix my eyes on the deer head across from us. The ceiling above it has water stains from leaks and one tile sagging. This place could collapse any minute.

"I appreciate you saying you trust me. I would never do anything to hurt you. In fact, I'd protect you. I might not be political royalty, but one thing about rednecks is we know how to take care of people."

She half grins. "You're a good guy."

*Am I a good guy?* I lean forward and run my hand across my jaw. Marrying someone to get a new trailer doesn't speak well for my character.

I turn to her. "I want you to really think about all your options tonight. It's been a crazy day, and we've both had bad news. If there's any hesitation tomorrow, we don't need to do this. I can crash with buddies, get a cheap apartment, or sleep in the bed of my truck. Heck, I don't care. I'm not gonna marry you unless you're all in."

She tears up again. My face falls. "I've said something wrong."

She shakes her head. "No, that's so sweet." Her voice gets squeaky. "That's why I want to marry you."

I blink. Any other girl, and I'd think she was drunk. But Carmelita has the most solid head of anyone. Tears pool in her eyes. I lift the hand holding the napkin where we wrote the agreement.

She takes it and laughs, then blots her eyes before handing it back.

I stand and reach out my hand. She takes it, and I pull her to her feet.

"Tomorrow, I'll be here. Come by before noon if you really want to do this. If not, that's fine too. It's your decision." I lift the tear-stained napkin. "It's only a year."

She smiles. "A lot can happen in a year."

"That's why you need to think about this long and hard before we go to the courthouse."

She nods slowly.

I realize we're still holding hands and drop hers to open the door. She steps outside, and I follow her. I stand a few feet back and watch her get in her car and drive away.

The damp napkin chills against my hand, so I shove it in my shirt pocket. My heart beats faster with it balled against my chest. I climb the steps back to the door and go inside.

I've got some thinking to do too.

## CHAPTER FOUR

*Liam*

I rummage through the cabinets and find a bag of chips not yet stale. Tomorrow I'll either be married or heading home for the holidays. That was enough to justify not buying groceries yet.

I toss a handful of chips in my mouth and decide to take a shower. It's already eleven, which means my bride must've gotten cold feet. Just as well.

Worst case scenario, I can ask Daddy for more money to live on or try and take online classes. Of course, going online would mean having to co-op closer to home. And I hate asking Daddy for money. I feel like such a little kid. It's bad enough that Lacie got all these scholarships to pay for school, and they have to pay for all of mine.

There's got to be another alternative besides moving in with the ferret pervert.

After one more handful of chips, I chuck the bag in the trash. That last bite was stale.

My stomach growls as I head to the bathroom for a shower. One upside to this place is the hot water works most of the time. It just takes a bit to warm up.

I turn on the water while I undress and shave my face. Then I step around the rug in front of the tub to get in the shower. The rug covers a gaping hole in the floor. Kevin McCallister himself couldn't set a better trap.

The water trickles down my back and hits my hungry stomach when I turn around. I really should learn to cook something other than wild game meat. Somehow I've managed to exist on that, junk food, and takeout for the past four years. Whenever I go back home, I eat until I'm stuffed, like my mama's food is a last meal in prison.

I shower quickly, then dry my hair with a towel. Careful not to step on the rug, I tiptoe out and change into jeans in my room. As I pull on a sweatshirt someone knocks on my door.

Tiger walks in without knocking, and my other buddies usually text before they come. Either it's someone I don't know, or . . .

I hurry to the door and open it to Carmelita in a white dress. Her hair is curled, with a flower behind her ear. My mouth drops.

"If you changed your mind—"

I grab her hand and pull her inside. "Have a seat, I've got to finish getting ready."

She grins, and I rush to my room. *She's here to marry me, and she looks gorgeous.*

My hands shake as I unlock the gun safe. I'm almost certain I might need my birth certificate. I feel around the top shelf of the safe for the folder that holds that and other documents my parents make me keep. My hand lands on the tiny velvet box.

Nannie's ring.

I'd totally forgot about that. I open the box and pull out the diamond. Perfect. Fake marriage or not, she deserves something pretty for marrying me, and for being so pretty. I start to shove the ring in my pocket, then realize what I'm wearing.

I thumb through the nice shirts in the back of my closet and find a nice button-down, then change into pressed Wranglers instead of my work jeans. I put the ring in my jeans pocket and stare at my appearance in the dresser mirror. As I'm finger combing my hair, I remember that I forgot to brush my teeth.

A squeal comes from the bathroom right before I open the door.

Funny, I don't remember closing the door. I knock on it.

"Carmelita? Are you in there?"

"I'm stuck in the floor!"

"Oh shoot," I whisper.

The door is locked, so I turn sideways and hit it with my shoulder. It doesn't budge. I kick at it until it falls.

Carmelita stands in front of the shower, hands raised to cover her head. Thankfully, the door was so worn, it crumbled in two near the hallway.

"Sorry about that."

She drops her arms. "I had to use the restroom and was walking to the sink."

"Looks like you found the sinkhole."

Her eyes widen at her leg hung under a board.

"Here." I grab a towel and shove it between her leg and the board to protect it. Then I jerk the board back.

She steps out. "Thanks."

"You're welcome."

Without thinking, I lift her in my arms and carry her into the living room. I set her feet on the ground and scan her toe to head.

"You look pretty, by the way."

Her lip twitches. "Thanks."

I raise a finger. "Last chance to back out."

She shakes her head. "Nope. I really thought this through."

I take a deep breath, then exhale. She reaches for my hand. My palm closes around her much smaller one. The warmth of her touch shoots up my arm.

"Let's do this, then." I grin and lead her outside.

When I turn to lock my door, there's another paper taped to it. I rip off the second notice for condemning my trailer and roll my eyes. This time they didn't even bother to use an envelope.

Carmelita squeezes my hand. "That's why we're doing this."

I nod and walk to my truck. She breaks her hand from mine, and fear gushes over me. *Is she backing out?*

"Wait. Let me get my purse."

I sigh in relief as I watch her lock her car and walk to my truck with her purse. She isn't backing out on me.

We climb in the truck and buckle up. Our eyes meet when I turn my head to back up. I could be fooling myself, but she doesn't look scared. Her eyes have an odd emotion I can't read. Not that I've ever been good at reading women. However, I don't sense any fear or worry in her eyes. Maybe she won't regret this.

The only thing I'm regretting right now is not brushing my teeth.

## *Carmelita*

"There she is." I sigh in relief when I spot Janice on the courthouse steps.

"I can't believe I'm helping you go through with this," she says when we're within a few feet of her.

"It was your suggestion."

She shakes her head. "I hope it works well for you kids. He's a nice enough looking guy."

"Thanks." Liam smirks.

"Where's your witness?"

Liam hooks a thumb toward the building. "Inside. He already had to come here and renew his pistol permit."

"Ah, perfect." Janice smiles, then laughs.

The three of us enter the courthouse. My stomach flutters with nerves, but not in the way it does when I'm second-guessing myself. More in the way of I'm nervous about living with Liam.

I'm an only child who grew up in a massive home. Sharing a common kitchen area in a dorm was torture to me. Now I'm about to share a small home with a man I don't totally know. Will I be able to handle that?

In order to make the marriage believable, we need to live together. Janice made that clear. Besides, part of the agreement is so we'll both have a place to live.

"Dude!"

A short, stocky guy in a cowboy hat struts up to us. I almost laugh, as he's the polar opposite build of Liam. He stops a foot in front of us and plants his hands on his hips.

"I didn't believe you at first, but this looks legit."

Liam nods. "It's happening." He sticks out his hand and the cowboy shakes it. "Thanks for witnessing it."

"Are you kidding? Like I'd miss this!" He slaps Liam on the shoulder so hard he jumps.

"Carmelita, this is Tiger, my—"

"Best friend ever," Tiger interrupts.

He holds out his hand. I attempt to shake it, but he kisses my knuckles. Liam pulls him back.

"She's here to marry me, remember?"

Janice clears her throat and checks her watch. "I hate to break up the love fest, but I'm on my lunch break."

"Of course." I give her an apologetic smile and lead us toward the probate judge's office.

The secretary greets us.

"Hi, we need a marriage license, please," I say.

She narrows her gaze at our group. "Between whom? We only allow marriages for two people."

Liam chuckles. "Me and her." He wraps his arm around my shoulder.

"They are our witnesses," I clarify.

The lady swats a hand. "Oh, we done away with witnesses. Y'all just need to fill out a form and pay the fee."

"Great, I'm going to grab a sub and head back to the office. Call me when it's official, hon." Janice pats my back and hurries toward the exit.

Liam and I both turn to Tiger, who's grinning as the secretary goes to retrieve a form. He sways back and forth mindlessly before noticing our stares.

"What? Like I'd miss this?"

Liam sighs. "Sure, you can stay."

"Yes." Tiger pumps a fist in the air.

The secretary returns with a form and slides it across the counter to us. "Fill this out, show some identification, and you can pay in cash or check or money order."

Liam drops his arm from my shoulder and reaches for his wallet. I shiver slightly at the loss of warmth. I shouldn't have worn a lace dress in the dead of winter. Somehow I reasoned if my family ever finds out about this marriage, I can at least say I dressed properly for the occasion.

"Seventy-three dollars," the clerk says.

Liam thumbs through his wallet, then selects a card. "Better run it on this."

She frowns and takes the card skeptically. I select a pen from a nearby cupful and start filling out my portion of the form while Liam makes the transaction.

"I can pay you back for half," I whisper when he returns the card to his wallet.

"Don't worry about it. What's mine is yours in a few minutes anyway."

"Smooth," Tiger croons.

Neither of us acknowledge him. The clerk checks our IDs while we finish the form. Then she glances over it.

"Let me get the judge."

A well-dressed man comes out wiping his mouth with a napkin. "Looks like y'all get to be my first marriage after lunch." He chucks the napkin in a trash can and pulls at his belt.

We wait awkwardly for him to join us in the hallway. Then we fall in line when he walks toward the courtroom. He flips on the lights and leads us up front.

"We can make this sentimental or simple."

"Simple," Liam and I say together.

"Ah, man," Tiger mutters.

"All right, face one another." The judge clears his throat.

Liam and I turn inward and lock eyes. I always knew his eyes were blue, but I never knew how blue until now. They're the color of rare blue pearls. Like my favorite pearl I found as a child.

"You still okay?" he whispers.

"Yes." I smile to reassure him.

An odd sense of calm washes over me as I stare into his pearl eyes. I am okay, better than okay. I'm one hundred percent confident Liam is the perfect choice for this marriage.

The judge asks a few questions, to which we both agree. Tiger gets uncomfortably close to us and takes a photo. Liam grabs his phone and shoves it in his pocket.

"Do you have any rings?"

"No," I answer.

"I do," Liam says.

My eyes widen. We didn't discuss rings last night. The point seemed moot when compared to us brainstorming a place to live and ways to make money.

He digs his fist in his jeans pocket and pulls out a beautiful diamond solitaire. My eyes widen even more if that's possible. How and when did he have time to find a ring?

Liam takes my left hand in his and slides the ring up my finger. It's a little large and slides to one side.

"We can have it sized," he comments.

A small gasp escapes my mouth. I never expected a diamond ring from Liam. At best, I considered purchasing my own simple band to wear around work and sell the marriage. I don't have to worry about that now.

The judge pronounces us husband and wife. Liam smiles down at me. *Will he kiss me?*

My throat constricts. I hadn't thought this far ahead. I take a deep breath and decide I won't fight him off if he kisses me. After all, we need to act married in front of the judge.

Liam reaches over and gives me an awkward side hug like a middle school boy posing for a photo with his first crush. Then he extends a hand to the judge. The judge eyes his hand suspiciously before shaking it.

"Thanks for marrying us on short notice. Appreciate it."

"Sure, son. It's my job."

They break apart, and we leave the courtroom with Tiger on our tail. He throws an arm around both our shoulders.

"What's next? A honeymoon?"

"The mobile home festival," Liam answers.

Tiger drops his arms. "Dude, you can take her someplace more romantic than that. My grandma has a beach house. I might could hook you up with that."

Liam pulls Tiger's phone from his back pocket and deletes the photo he took of us. Tiger looks confused when he hands it back.

"Tiger, it's important not to post or tell this everywhere. Carmelita and I don't want our families knowing just yet."

He stares at us blankly.

"Got it?" Liam asks in a harsher tone.

"Yes, sir." Tiger salutes him, knocking his hat sideways.

Liam frowns, then Tiger straightens. "For real, man. I won't say anything."

"Good." Liam glances at both of us. "All I've had today is some old potato chips. I'll gladly take you two to lunch to celebrate, if that's acceptable."

I smile. "Only if I pay."

Liam opens his mouth to protest, but I cover it with my hand. "What's yours is mine, remember?"

He doesn't say another word. I slide my hand away from his mouth and try to forget the way his lips felt against it. Or the way the diamond ring on my finger looked beneath his pearl-blue eyes.

As we head to his truck, I mentally remind myself this is a marriage of *convenience*. The only convenience in having an attractive husband is so others will believe us—not me.

# CHAPTER FIVE

*Liam*

Maybe it's a good sign that the mobile home festival starts the weekend after our wedding. I wake up to my neighbor sticking a For Sale sign in front of his trailer. He waves at me after hammering it into the ground.

He's written "$3500 OBO" sloppily across the sign. I doubt he'll get that, since his was marked to be condemned too, but I admire his effort.

Carmelita pulls up right on time. I lock the door behind me and hurry down the steps. I knock on her window, and she rolls it down.

"I can drive," I tell her.

"My car will get better gas. Especially since we're going to Mobile."

"It's in Montgomery."

"But it's the Mobile home festival."

I chuckle. "No, that's pronounced Mo-Bill."

"Ohhh." She blushes, then rolls up her window and gets out.

We get in my truck and head for the interstate. It's odd thinking that we've officially been married for a few days but haven't seen one another since then. We've texted about logistics of things, but nothing more.

"Did you hear from your work?"

"Yeah." She smiles. "They're filing things so I can start first of the year."

"That's awesome."

She smiles wider. "Did you ever get more details on why they're condemning your place?"

I shake my head. "Something about rebranding the park as upscale."

"Oh."

"So we gotta get something super nice." I raise my eyebrows up and down.

She laughs.

We talk about what we both want in the new home. My list is more along the lines of a comfy couch and big-screen TV. Carmelita cares more about the floor plan and kitchen appliances. I assume real couples have the same priorities.

I reach for my sunglasses when the sun hits the windows. Nannie's ring twinkles in the light. It looks good on Carmelita's finger. So good that it scares me a little.

Does she wear it when we're not together? Even in her dorm room? I shouldn't care, but I do.

She catches me staring at her, and I hurriedly put on my glasses. The light turns green, and I make the last turn before our destination.

We barely drive a mile when I spot a huge vinyl Pepsi sign that reads, "Mobile Home Festival."

## QUEEN OF MY DOUBLE-WIDE TRAILER

Trucks, trailers, and vehicles of all sizes line the gravel road ahead. I drive several yards, then realize we best park where we can. I pull onto the side of the road, leaving enough room to get out.

I have no expectations for today other than to leave having purchased a new home. The sooner we find what we need, the better.

"It's more crowded than I imagined," Carmelita comments.

"No kidding." I get out and she follows.

We walk down the road that ends at a field. As many trailers as are in my mobile home park sit in rows with people mingling around them. Only these trailers are all new and shiny. No rusty hardware or broken underpinning.

They light up like angelic rectangles in the sunlight. Carmelita's lips curve as she scans the field. No doubt, she's comparing them to my current place.

An older couple sits behind a table at the entrance to the field, taking up money. I reach for my wallet as we approach them.

"Five-dollar admission."

"Yes, sir." I hand him a ten.

The woman smiles and tears off two armbands. I put mine on, then hand Carmelita hers. Instead of taking it, she holds her arm steady. I wrap it around her wrist and notice the ring twisting on her finger.

"We can get that sized."

"It's fine." She wiggles the armband while we walk past the entrance.

"No, the ring. It's big."

She holds her hand up and admires it. My heart beats faster. It's the least I could give her for buying me a new home.

"Where should we go first?"

Carmelita drops her hand and scans the area. "I guess we can start at one end and keep walking."

"Sounds like a plan." I lift my hand, signaling her to go first.

Every trailer along the way has someone showing it. Carmelita and I stroll past the first row, peeking inside the open doors. A familiar voice echoes behind me. I turn and find Jeffrey discussing a whirlpool tub with a woman.

I grab Carmelita's arm and pull her inside the mobile home beside us.

"Whoa. You scared me for a minute. You could've just said you wanted to go in this one."

I pull us away from the window and whisper in her ear, "The guy out there is my aunt's ex. He doesn't need to see us here."

Her eyes bug. "Oh."

I move the rose-colored curtain to the side and watch Jeffrey get closer to the woman. She waves a hand our direction. Maybe she's coming in here and leaving him.

I'm halfway correct.

They walk *together* toward our trailer. I gasp and grab Carmelita's hand. We head down the hallway before they make it up the front steps.

"Why are you acting like we're hiding?"

"Because we are," I whisper-yell. "He's coming inside."

"The jets on this tub are more powerful. I put one similar in my home." Jeffrey's voice booms louder with every breath.

I pull Carmelita into a room and shut the door, then lock it. She steps away, while I double-check the lock.

"Uh, what if they try and come in here?"

"What makes you say that?"

I hear her but don't see her. Then she steps out of a door

and motions me over. Past the oversized bed is an en-suite master bath, complete with a garden tub.

Our eyes meet just before the bedroom door handle jiggles.

"Hide."

This time it's Carmelita who pulls me behind a door. We stand in the bathroom breathing heavily. Thanks to the thin walls, I can hear Jeffrey loud and clear.

"I've got a key."

I swallow and squeeze Carmelita's hand. The voices grow closer, and she pulls me to the edge of the bathroom. There's one more door.

Carmelita opens it and screams to the top of her lungs. I assume it's a spider or possum until I hear another scream. I peek over her head and see my Aunt Misty sitting on the toilet.

I'm officially scarred for life.

"Holy crap, Aunt Misty?"

She breathes heavily and stands. Luckily, her leather skirt covers everything we don't need to see. Unless you count her panties, which are around her ankles.

"What are you doing here?" she asks between breaths.

"Shopping for a new home. What are you doing here?"

"I'm singing as part of the entertainment and needed to pee. Jeffrey's always bragging about the bathrooms in his trailers, and you know how I feel about port-a-potties." She snarls her nose.

"You know this isn't hooked up to plumbing, right?"

She glances behind her, then winces. Then she faces us with a mischievous smirk. "Serves him right for skimping on child support."

Carmelita steps closer to me, and Misty smiles at her.

"Who's this lovely lady?"

"Carmelita."

"What an exotic name." Misty holds out a hand.

The struggle is evident on Carmelita's face. She doesn't want to be rude, nor does she want to shake the hand of someone who's using the bathroom.

After an awkward second, she waves at Misty. Just long enough for her to spot Nannie's ring. Misty grabs Carmelita's hand and holds it to her face.

"OMG. This is gorgeous! Did he give you that?"

Carmelita and I exchange glances. What do we say?

As if it couldn't get more awkward, Jeffrey walks in with the customer. When he sees us, we step away from the door, revealing Misty.

"Misty! What in tarnation are you doing here? I told you to quit coming by my place dropping your panties."

"I had to pee, and I'll have you know I haven't dropped my panties around you since I married Woody." Misty sticks her nose in the air and slams the door.

I jolt. The customer taps the side of the tub and turns to Jeffrey. "I may stop back by. I want to look around first."

She hurries toward the door with Jeffrey on her heels.

Jeffrey rushes back after losing the sale and turns on me.

"Boy, what are you doing here? You and—" He eyes Carmelita. "Hello, young lady."

She grips my arm and snuggles next to me.

"They're getting hitched," Misty calls from behind the door.

"What?" Jeffrey grins at me, then looks at Carmelita like she's crazy.

The bathroom door opens, and Misty struts out. "Excuse me." She stops at the sink and attempts to turn on the water. She pouts when nothing comes out.

"You getting married, son?"

"Uh, I want to buy a trailer."

He slaps my shoulder so hard it tingles. "Well, you come to the right place. Let ole Uncle Jeffrey hook you up."

"Ex-uncle," Misty corrects.

"Why aren't you with Woody?" Jeffrey snaps back.

"He's in the food truck line for Taco and Belle."

"Taco Bell has a food truck?" Carmelita asks.

"No, they're chihuahuas," I tell her.

She wrinkles her forehead.

"Not the food, the dogs are named Taco and Belle."

She lifts her chin, as if trying to make sense of it. I start to explain further, but Woody enters with Taco and Belle on matching leashes, wearing matching sweaters.

"There you are. I got us some barbecue at the truck." He waves to us. "Pleasure seeing all y'all."

Jeffrey and I mumble greetings.

"Thank you, dear." Misty goes to Woody and taps her cheek.

He plants a kiss on it. "You're welcome. I also ironed the fringe on your pink Dolly Parton jacket."

"Who's Dolly Parton?" Carmelita asks.

All three of us stare at her like she's grown an extra head.

"I can't believe I married someone who's never heard of Dolly Parton."

"Married?" Woody shouts.

I slap a hand across my mouth, then run it through my hair. So much for keeping this a secret from my family.

*Carmelita*

Yesterday was eventful, to say the least.

Having only given Jeffrey verbal agreement on the trailer, we walked around a while longer and compared it to others. Oddly enough, that home was the best. We put in an offer, and it's getting delivered today.

I pull up to Liam's lot and find him dragging a recliner down the front steps of the old trailer. Boxes line the edge of the street beside where I park.

"What are you doing?"

"Moving stuff out so they can come get this place."

A deer head stares at me from one of the boxes, causing me to flinch.

"Did you not want a storage unit?"

He grunts while moving the chair down the last step. "Seemed like a waste since it's happening this fast."

"You could've stored it at my dorm."

"Nah, the new place will be here in no time."

No sooner than he finishes that statement, a loud truck booms behind us. We turn to an eighteen-wheeler with a cab that's seen better days. It stops in front of the trailer, and a familiar face hangs out the window.

"Is that Jeffrey?"

Liam nods. "He repos these things. Giving him this one is how we got such a sweet deal."

I watch a bent sheet of metal blow up and down on the bottom of the home. The wind blows a little harder and it falls to the ground.

"What could he possibly want with this?"

"If he can't resell it, he'll salvage it for scrap metal."

"Okay . . ."

"That's my main business. I started freelancing as a salesman for new modular homes when they went up on child support. Dang Misty."

We both turn to Jeffrey, not realizing he was listening. Not that it matters.

Liam wipes his brow. "Jeffrey, if you don't mind helping me take this recliner to the road, you can haul off the home and everything in it."

"All right." He hops out and helps Liam move it beside the boxes.

Liam winces when Jeffrey drops his side on the curb a little too hard. The chair almost falls over and the legs pop open.

"Okay, Jeffrey, do your thing." Liam pulls me from the yard toward the recliner and boxes. "Stay in the safe zone."

My stomach flutters for a second. He doesn't have to care for my well-being, but he does. That reassures me he will look out for my best interests.

Jeffrey lights a cigarette and pulls the eighteen-wheeler into the yard. Two guys hop out the back door and start hooking things to the trailer. One is dressed head to toe in black, with a hoodie covering most of his face. The other is wearing a shirt with the sleeves cut off like it isn't December.

I stand safely beside Liam as they lift the trailer and place some wheel attachments beneath it, then hook them to the cab of the truck.

Jeffrey walks a straight line to the road and kicks a stump at the edge of the yard. He rubs his jaw, then goes to the truck. A few minutes later, he has built a ramp over the stump out of the fallen metal and wood.

We move closer to the lot beside us and watch in awe as they squeeze the trailer through the tight space in the road without hitting anything. This masterful performance isn't what I expected from a middle-aged guy who's wearing a baseball jersey.

He pulls into the center of the road and parks the truck. The two men who helped hook it up climb inside, while

Jeffrey climbs out. He collects the metal and wood used to make a ramp and tosses it inside the trailer. Then he flicks his cigarette in the ditch and exhales a long puff of smoke.

"Nice lot. Plenty of room for the new beauty you bought."

"Thanks," Liam says.

Liam's negotiation skills were a pleasant surprise. He made an offer on the show home out of urgency for needing it right away. However, in doing so, he struck a deal with Jeffrey to leave it furnished. That took care of a lot of our basics.

Jeffrey extends a hand, and Liam shakes it. He reaches out to hug me, but I curl into Liam. Luckily, he gets the hint and backs down.

"Pleasure doing business with y'all. I'll catch you later this month at Dirty Santa."

He returns to the truck and drives off, honking the horn. A few dogs howl and bark in the distance. I watch him drive away, then turn to Liam. My face is close to his chest. I step back, realizing I'm still snuggled to him.

"What's Dirty Santa?"

"Let's hope you don't have to find out."

I open my mouth to say I still want to know when his phone rings.

"Hello?"

He walks toward the edge of the lot where I can't hear the conversation. I stay near the neighbor's yard to give him privacy. That is until the neighbor steps out back in his underwear.

I tiptoe closer to the road in time for the new home to turn down our street. My jaw drops when I see it cut in half. Plastic tarps cover what should be the living room wall as if our home is a plate of leftovers. Is this Jeffrey's idea of getting something "half off"? I hurry to warn Liam.

I stop a few feet behind him and wait until he finishes what he's saying on the phone.

"No, it's not like that. I'm doing her a favor. We're really married, but not really a couple. It doesn't mean anything."

My stomach bottoms out, and my head gets fuzzy. What he said is true. We're not a couple. We're barely friends, more acquaintances. But hearing out loud that I'm in a meaningless marriage does something to me.

If my parents find out what I've done, I'll be the talk of the island. And not in a good way, especially when they find out my main motivation was to dodge Antonio. Mr. Coveted Bachelor of Oval Island.

I wrap my arms around my waist and walk toward the edge of our lot that backs up to some trees. It's the only place I feel safe from getting hit by a home, dissed by Liam, or flashed by the neighbor.

"Hey."

I turn to Liam walking toward me.

"Sorry about that. My mama heard about the marriage from Woody and called. I explained what's going on."

I swallow the lump in my throat. "She's fine with it?"

He scratches his head. "Fine as she can be, I guess. She said not to tell Daddy about it yet. At least now she understands why I haven't come home yet."

I nod and try not to frown. I've cut into his family time. The truck beeps, and I refocus my worry on the mobile home.

"Did you see that Jeffrey cut our house in half?" I point to the open wall, barely covered.

Liam chuckles. "All double-wides come in like that."

"They do?"

"Yeah, the other half should be coming, and they'll piece it together on site."

"Oh." I blink.

Liam drapes his arm around my shoulder. "You have a lot to learn about the South, Mrs. Sanderson."

I freeze. On paper, my last name is still Lim, but I'm also legally Liam's wife. It's hard enough to process that reality alone.

And even harder to navigate how we will pull this off for a full year without hurting two families.

## CHAPTER SIX

*Liam*

It's late afternoon by the time they finish connecting the two sides of the home. I pick up the first box and head for the front door.

The installation guy stops me there. "Whoa, what are you doing?"

"Moving in."

He shakes his head. "Not until we finish the roof and have everything inspected."

"But the water and power are hooked up."

"Doesn't matter. You can't go against regulations. It will take a few days at best."

"A few days?"

"Yeah, we gotta make sure your marriage line is settled."

"Oh, we're already married, if that's what you're asking."

The man chuckles and rubs his beard. "Son, I don't care

about y'all's business. I'm talking about the joints holding this place in one piece."

I glance back at Carmelita. She frowns. We were both looking forward to sleeping in our own bed tonight—separate beds and rooms, of course.

"We can take everything to the dorm."

I nod. "Guess we have no other choice."

I backtrack and put the box in the back seat of my truck. We do the same with all my other boxes. Her stuff is packed up, but still at the dorm. The installer is kind enough to help me load the recliner in the bed of the truck.

"I'll see if Tiger can help us unload it."

"If we can get it inside the dorm. I live on the top floor in a small space."

I rub my chin. "We'll think of something."

By the time we make it to the dorm, Tiger is waiting in the parking lot.

"How's the honeymooners?"

Carmelita blushes, even though we've engaged in zero honeymoon activities. This will be our first night under the same roof. My body tenses at that realization. No more walking around in my underwear and leaving the toilet seat up. I have to act better than I did at my parents' house. Whatever made my sister Lacie mad, I should assume Carmelita won't like.

And what a long list that is . . .

"Dude, I don't think this will fit." Tiger is in the bed of my truck, sitting in the recliner.

"Well, I've got to put it someplace. That's my most prized possession."

"That's sad," Carmelita comments.

She has a good point.

"Why don't I store it at the house until y'all move in the new place?"

"And let party people destroy it?"

Tiger jerks forward, slamming the legs shut. "I'll put it in a storage room. Most everyone is gone home anyway."

I sigh. "It's not like I have a choice if I want to keep it."

I open the back door of my truck and start unloading boxes. Carmelita does as well, leaving Tiger alone in the back of my truck.

We walk to the dorm entrance, and I shuffle boxes to get the door. Carmelita passes by, and I follow her to the elevators. We ride to the top floor in silence, holding our boxes. When we're in her small living room, I'm certain the recliner won't fit.

"If you want to organize your things, I can make Tiger help me with the rest of the boxes."

"Thanks."

I nod and return to the truck. Tiger hasn't moved with the exception of closing his eyes. I slap the side of the truck, making him jolt. He curses and pops open his eyes.

"Sleeping on the job?"

"Just trying to live up to what you're paying me."

"Help me with the rest of these boxes, please."

"Well, if the man says 'please' . . ."

He stands and stretches, then leaps over the side of the truck at an impressive height for someone no more than five and a half feet. We stack boxes so high that Tiger has to peek around the corner of his armful. I open the door to the building and lead him to the elevator. Two girls get out when the elevator door opens.

"Ladies," Tiger greets them.

They smile and step around us. If this had been a week ago, I might've greeted them too. But I'm a married man now. Even if it's a marriage on paper only, I have to honor that. What's strange is that I didn't care to say hello.

Maybe I'll come out of this marriage a changed man, no

longer attracted to women like Bambi. That would be an added bonus to the obvious benefit of having a home.

Carmelita's dorm door is closed, so I knock. She opens it and moves for us to deliver the boxes. I ask where she wants them since some are heavier. I also take note of her couch being short. If only my recliner would fit.

"I'll be back after we take the chair," I say.

"I'll be here." She half smiles and picks up more boxes.

We glance at one another like we've done the last few days whenever we part. Like we're unsure how to say bye. Do we hug, shake hands? Not wanting to accidentally cross an undeclared line, I nod and exit the dorm. Tiger tips his hat and follows me.

"Dude, the tension between you two was epic."

I push the elevator button and stare at the doors.

"I know you heard me," he continues.

The door opens to nobody this time. If only a hot girl would pop out to change Tiger's one-track mind. We step inside, and I lean against the back wall.

"Liam, what's going on with you two?"

I scowl at him. "Nothing. We're technically married on paper, that's all."

"Sure didn't look like all. Last time a woman looked at me that way . . . Let's just say I didn't walk away."

I sigh and straighten the cap on my head.

"She likes you."

I frown at him.

"I can tell."

"Since you're such an expert on relationships." Tiger's an even bigger flirt than me and way less interested in settling down.

"Never claimed to be, but I am an expert on women."

The elevator doors open to an older woman. "Afternoon,

ma'am." Tiger tips his hat, and the woman smiles. He winks at me after we pass her. I shake my head.

While I'm opening my truck door, Tiger jumps over the back and plops in the recliner.

"Get up front."

"Nope. It's not far. This can be my payment for helping."

"Fine." I groan and get inside.

I drive slowly out of respect for my recliner—not Tiger. He waves at the few cars we pass like he's homecoming king of a one-car parade. I park around back of the frat house.

Tiger stands up and knocks on my rear window. "Back up to the door," he yells once he has my attention.

I back up and come to a sudden stop, laughing when he hits the floor. Serves his cocky self right.

"Dude." He stands and slaps his hat back on his head.

"My bad." I laugh harder, then open the tailgate.

Tiger jumps down and opens the back door to the house. "There's a storage room right down the hall from here."

"Thanks."

We unload it, and I walk backward until he tells me to stop. The storage room is more of a junk room for broken sports equipment and party supplies.

"And nobody will bother it here?"

"Not before you need it."

Tiger plops down again when we set it on the floor. He reclines, kicks the legs up, and rests his hands behind his head.

"Looks like you're ready to protect it."

He smirks. "You dodged my question earlier."

"What question?"

"About the honeymoon."

"If you're referring to the wedding night, she went back to her place and I went back to mine. I ate a Hot Pocket and went to bed."

"Seriously?"

"I may have eaten some ice cream too. Can't remember."

Tiger moans. "If I were married to a hot girl, the last thing I'd think about was what I had for supper."

"I told you, it's not like that with us."

Tiger unfolds his arms and rises up. "Maybe it should be."

I shrug and stare at the broken basketball goal across the room. Tiger is staring at me when I drop my gaze. He opens his hands as if wanting an answer.

I'd be lying if I said I hadn't imagined something more. Every day that passes, I have to talk myself down from suggesting she hang out a little longer. Part of me hopes to one day hang out all night. After all, it's not like we'd be breaking any morals. Legally, we belong together in every way.

"She doesn't think of me that way." That's the most truthful answer I can give.

"You sure about that, bro?"

I cup my hand around the bill of my cap and consider Tiger's question. He's such an idiot, I seriously doubt he's picked up on something I haven't.

But I'm sure as heck going to pay better attention.

*Carmelita*

I plate the chicken on top of a bed of rice and take a long whiff. Cooking my favorite family dish brings back nostalgic memories. If I close my eyes, I'm back in my mama's kitchen, preparing a family meal with her and my lola. Everything is perfect until Antonio's family comes over for dinner.

Even my memories get ruined by him.

Good thing I'm not next door to his family's property, but in my dorm.

The dorm I now share with my husband. As nervous as I am about sharing a close space with Liam, I'm excited to cook for someone besides myself.

Not long after he returned from storing the recliner, I went grocery shopping. With so few people left in the dorm, I can have free rein of the kitchen.

I clean up after myself, then carry our plates to my suite. The door is cracked, and I peek inside. Liam is on the couch watching TV. I toe the edge of the door and open it with my foot.

"That smells awesome."

I've barely made it across the room when he compliments the dish. My cheeks flush. Not everyone appreciates our spiced foods, and some of the other residents would complain about me cooking them.

Liam pulls two bottles of water from the mini fridge while I set the plates on the table.

"When you said you were cooking dinner, I expected a frozen pizza or something."

I laugh. "I love to cook. It's something Mama and Lola and me all did together."

He smiles. "My mama and sister cook together."

When he mentions his mom, I try not to think about the phone conversation I overheard. He said it wasn't an issue, but I can't imagine any mom wanting her son to marry under such circumstances.

"Water?"

I snap out of my worry enough to notice the bottle of water he's holding out.

"Thanks." I sit in one of the two chairs at my tiny table.

Liam sits across from me. He picks up his fork and stares at his plate. "What am I eating?"

"Chicken adobo."

"Chicken what?"

"Ah-doh-bo," I pronounce.

He shrugs and takes a big bite. After a few chews, his eyes roll back and he sighs. "This is awesome," he says around a mouthful of food.

"Thanks." My heart beats faster as Liam scoops up more of my favorite food.

I'd forgotten the joy of sharing my meal with someone else. Whenever I eat with coworkers or girls in the dorm, it's always takeout or tailgate food. There's little pleasure in cooking an entire meal to eat alone in my room.

"Your roommate is lucky."

"I didn't have one my last year. After she graduated, I requested a single-suite room."

"No, I mean me." He grins.

My cheeks warm at the compliment. I'm also keenly aware of his choice of wording. *Roommate*. That's the most accurate way to describe our setup.

I'm wearing a ring, but can probably make a solid argument for keeping my last name. We will both have engineering careers, and I can use the excuse of my culture. Not many women on the island choose to keep their maiden names, but nobody here will know. And it's not like we'll sleep in the same room.

I squirm in my seat at the suggestion of sharing a room, much less a bed, with Liam. More than anything else, that's what makes our marriage different.

"I'm sorry the place is so small. You can have my bed."

Liam's forehead wrinkles. "Why are you apologizing? At least this place is nice." He wipes his mouth with a paper towel and glances around my tiny living room area. "You literally fell through the floor at my old place."

I snicker. "True."

"And there's no way I'm letting you give me your bed. I'll be fine sleeping in here."

I blink. "My couch is a love seat half your height." My stomach buckles at the word "love seat." Why do Americans call it that stupid name?

"So I'll make a space on the floor."

"You can have any extra blankets or pillows you need."

"That offer, I'll accept." He smiles and polishes off his plate.

I finish my food a few minutes later and start to stand. He places his hand on my arm, sending a shiver up my body.

"This may sound redneck, but do you mind if I eat the rest of your food?"

I look at the few bites left on my plate, then to him. "No, go ahead."

He moves his hand from my arm and takes the paper plate. I make a mental note to buy more ingredients as soon as we move into the mobile home.

Liam eats everything left in two bites. I throw away our empty plates and put away the spices I used for the chicken.

"Do you mind if I take a shower?" Liam asks.

"No, go ahead. I'll show you where everything is."

I lead him to the small bathroom across from my bedroom and open the closet.

"Here's the towels. I have my soap and shampoo in a box. I'll get that."

"Me too."

We turn to leave at the same time, and I bump into his chest. I tilt my head, and our eyes meet. He takes a deep breath in, then exhales. I stand, frozen in front of him, our bodies a centimeter away.

"You smell good. Can I use your shampoo and soap?" he whispers.

I nod, then slide past him and hurry to my room, where I drug all my boxes. My heart beats against my chest as I dig for my toiletries. My Japanese Cherry Blossom shower gel is at the bottom beside my volume-enhancing shampoo. Two items I'm certain Liam's never used. Not to stereotype, but he looks like someone who would use an all-purpose Suave product.

"Here you go," I say, walking to the bathroom.

He takes the products from me and sets them on the side of the shower, then rips off his shirt. I stay a second longer than I should and watch his slim yet cut back, as the shirt slides up to his head. Then I hurry back to my room before he notices I'm still there.

I lie on my bed and stare at the ceiling. What is wrong with me? I can't gawk at my phony husband. I blame it on my lifestyle. The last five years, I buckled down and did nothing but study and work. Everything I did was to one day move back to the island and work in the gem industry.

Until last year, when I went home for the holidays. Antonio cornered me at a party and stuck a blue pearl and diamond ring in my face. The same color blue as Liam's eyes.

My skin crawls remembering that day. We weren't even together at the time. We haven't been "together" since high school. He gave a long speech about how we were destined for one another and he wanted to make it official. I gave the long distance and still in college excuse to back him down.

That bought me time.

If I go back this year, I can't blame it on school. My only alibi will be starting a job in the states—and marrying Liam, of course.

But God knows I'm not ready for the family drama that will create.

## CHAPTER SEVEN

*Liam*

"Star?" I wrinkle my forehead as I study the bag of brown pods.

"They're a spice," Carmelita answers as she lays the bag in the buggy.

"They look like sweet gum balls."

She laughs. "Trust me, they add lots of flavor."

I shrug. "I trust you."

Her cheeks pinken before she turns her attention back to the spices.

We both made a grocery list for the trailer. Mine is mostly sweet tea, Mountain Dew, and snack foods. So I'll gladly default to her for the cooking. Tonight will be our first night in the new home.

For the last few days, we've shared her dorm. I'd like to think we've become closer, even though she would go into her office a few hours a day, training for her new job. I would try and stay busy to keep from admitting that I missed her. I fixed two loose doorknobs and unclogged her bathroom sink. I also noticed her closet was extremely organized and made a mental note to put an organizer in her new closet.

Not that I'd admit that I went in her closet. As far as Carmelita knows, I've never set foot in her bedroom. I'd like to keep it that way . . . unless she invites me there.

But we're nowhere near that. If anything, she sees me as a friend now, rather than some not-so-smart guy she tutors.

"Let's get some closet organizers," I suggest.

"Closet organizers?"

"Yeah, you know, those wire or wooden shelves and cubbies. I thought you might like some in the closets, since women like those things."

She narrows her eyes. "Have you been in a lot of women's closets?"

My neck heats up. I can't confess to snooping in her room, and I don't want to imply that I've been in a lot of other women's rooms.

"I have a sister."

She nods. "Makes sense."

My body untenses. I managed to wiggle out of that one without lying.

She smirks and grabs a few more items I've never heard of. My family's main ingredient for meals is butter.

"Let's go check out the organizers before we get the cold stuff."

I nod and follow her toward the home section. She smiles at a row of candles and photo frames. Her fingers graze some knickknack things made of wood.

"While we're here, you could pick out some stuff you like."

"Yeah, I've got my list too."

Carmelita holds up a paper with much better handwriting than mine. It's filled with ingredients and toiletry items, and a few cooking items.

"No, not necessities." I lean across the end of the buggy and look her in the eye. "What's something you want? Something you couldn't have in a dorm?"

She stares up for a bit, then an entire smile takes over her face. "A rice cooker."

"Rice cooker?"

"Yeah."

I let go of the buggy and rub my chin. "My mama cooks rice in a normal pot."

She lifts then lowers one shoulder. "I guess it is kind of silly once I think of it. We just always had one back home."

She turns down the next aisle to the organizers. I catch up to her and touch her arm. She stares up at me.

"It's not silly. I want you to have a rice cooker."

One corner of her mouth ticks up.

"I'm serious. It's not silly. I've never heard of one is all." I move my hand slightly up and down her arm.

Her eyes land on it, but she doesn't move. My hand tingles at her acknowledgment of my touch. I slowly remove it and straighten my cap. "So organizers. Wood or metal?"

"Handyman's choice." She smirks at me.

I try not to laugh at an older man wearing nothing but overalls and slippers digging in a sale bin behind us. Never a dull moment at Walmart.

"What's so funny?"

I nod behind her. The old man bends at the waist, putting the baggy bottom of his overalls on full display. She grins. "Did I ever tell you this is my favorite store?"

"Seriously?" I laugh.

"Yeah, we have nothing like this back home. All the things you need in one place, and all the—" She waves her arm toward the old man, who's now examining a back scratcher. "Interesting people."

I loop my arm around her shoulder and chuckle. "If you like Walmart, darling, you're gonna love Paul's place."

"Paul's place?"

"Yeah, the General Store in Wisteria. When we—" I clamp my mouth shut and slide my arm out from around her. "I mean, you know, if you want to go there sometime. You don't have to. I understand if you're going home for Christmas."

"Uh . . ." She studies the box on an organizer kit for a moment. "I can't go home this year."

"Why not?"

"I haven't exactly told them about me getting a job here, or . . ." She raises her left hand and wiggles her ring finger.

I raise one brow.

"I know your family found out, but mine still hasn't. Explaining why I got a permanent job here will be hard enough, but explaining why I married you . . ." She sighs.

I cross my arms and frown. "What's wrong with me? Is it because I'm not that smart or not that rich or not that Asian?"

"It's because you're not Antonio."

"Is that a club or religion?"

She cackles so loudly that she knocks over a rack of curtain rods. I admire her joyful face until she bends to pick up her mess. I kneel and hand her a stack of rods. "Here."

Our eyes meet, and her face goes serious. I focus on her gaze and watch her swallow. Everything around me freezes for a split second, as if we're not in the middle of Walmart, with weird shirtless overall men running around and nineties pop music playing in the background.

She licks her lips and my stomach curls. I halfway hope

she's going to kiss me. Instead, she whispers, "Antonio is my ex-boyfriend."

I drop a rod and wince when it dings on the floor.

"Our families have a long history. His dad runs our island, and his dad did before that, and his dad before that, and many more." She sighs even louder.

I tighten my grip on the one rod I'm still holding.

"He's an only child, and so am I. My parents and his parents have this idea that we're meant to end up together." Her eyes go glossy like she's about to cry.

"And that's why you want to stay here?"

"I like Alabama more than I thought I would, but yeah."

My legs numb a bit, so I sit back on the floor. Carmelita sits beside me. A woman pushes a buggy in front of us. I move the few rods still on the floor out of her way, and Carmelita slides closer to me until our sides are touching.

I relax my shoulders against the bottom shelf filled with towels. Her slim leg and shoulder warm my left side. Despite the cold, hard floor and people shuffling about, I could sit like this all night.

"I don't know what it's like where you grew up, but people can be like that. My sister kinda went through that with our county sheriff a while back."

Her face is a mixture of surprise and confusion.

"Anyway, the good news is she married the man she wanted to marry, and he's even friends with the sheriff now."

"Sounds like a fairy-tale ending."

A slow smile creeps across her face, causing me to smile too. We both burst out laughing. After a good long laugh, she rests her left hand on my knee. "We should probably finish shopping."

My heart beats faster looking at my ring on her hand. She gives my leg a gentle pat, then slides her hand away and stands. That same hand lands in front of my face. I take it and stand, pretending that she helps me up.

She smiles before dropping my hand and grabbing the organizer kit she was eyeing earlier. I hold one end and read the box. "I think we need a bigger one for your closet."

"This should be fine for the second bedroom."

I put the box back on the shelf and put a larger one in the buggy. "You, my wife, are getting the master bedroom. I will take the spare."

A hint of a tear flickers in the corner of her eye.

"I know marrying me isn't your fairy tale, but I promise to do whatever I can to make this year a good one. I'll be whatever you need to make sure you one day get your fairy tale."

She nods and her eyes moisten. I dab the edge of her eyelid with my thumb and wipe away a falling tear. My heart beats faster, and it takes everything in me not to kiss her.

Needing something to do with my hands to keep them away from her, I take the buggy and start walking toward the frozen foods with my wife beside me.

*Carmelita*

"You've already met the worst of them with Woody and Aunt Misty. At least when it comes to actual family members," Liam assures me.

I grip my coffee cup tighter and watch more trees go by. We've passed an awful lot of forests, even on the interstate.

"Who besides family will be there?"

My nerves twitch, and I take a long drag of my coffee. I try my best to focus as Liam spouts out a roll call of names.

"The sheriff I told you about, Bradley, Lacie's ex. But all is cool in that situation now. Then there's the family whose road connects to ours. They have like seven kids now, or maybe eight, so I don't remember all their names." Liam thumps the steering wheel. "Oh, and I can't forget Paul."

"The guy with the store."

"Yeah. He shows up everywhere anytime there's food."

I nod. "Sounds like a lot of people."

"That's just at G-Maw's Christmas gathering. There will be even more when we do the progressive dinner."

"What's that?"

"We start out at my parents' house for appetizers, then eat at G-Maw's, then dessert at Aunt Carla's."

"That sounds like a lot of traveling for one meal."

He chuckles. "We all live on the same road."

"Oh."

Liam seems to know and have a connection with everyone. Maybe a small town in Alabama isn't too far off from a small island in the Pacific.

"Then there's the Christmas morning hog killing. It draws a whole different crowd."

"Like Lechon."

"Huh?"

"We roast a suckling pig over an open fire on special occasions."

Liam smiles at me. "Then you'll fit in just fine."

"Have you brought a girl to your family events before?"

Liam palms the back of his neck. I watch as he stares at the road ahead. When we come to a red light, he turns to me. I raise my brows.

"G-Maw gets too excited whenever we bring someone.

You wouldn't really do that unless you're already serious about them."

I lift my chin. "So you haven't had a serious girlfriend?"

He shakes his head. "You?"

"No, I haven't had a girlfriend."

Liam narrows his eyes at my sarcasm before focusing back on the road.

"Antonio was my only relationship. If you could call it that."

"What do you mean?"

I pick at the lid on my coffee cup. "I always viewed him as more of a friend. We sort of fell into dating during high school, and he took it way more serious than me."

"Then you planned an escape to rural Alabama." Liam glances at me and smirks.

I laugh. "Not the way I'd put it, but technically true."

We turn off onto a smaller road. A sign in the distance reads, "Welcome to Apple Cart."

"Are those apple trees?"

"Yep."

At least the name makes sense. We pass through a tiny town with a bank, the General Store that Liam mentioned, and a few more buildings. A giant blow-up Santa waves to us from on top of the grocery store. A minute later, we're back to trees and fields.

A sign on plastic pipes, with one side falling, reads, "Welcome to Wisteria." It's followed shortly by a Waffle House.

"This is where you live?"

"Yep. Lucky for you, we live before you get to the county line."

"Why?"

"That's where Inn The Hole Enchilada is."

"In the what?" I scrunch my brow.

"It's one of those shopping-center-type buildings with

three businesses. A motel, a liquor store, and a Mexican joint. Quality Inn never fixed the 'Quality' on their sign, so we call the place Inn The Hole Enchilada."

I blink and Liam laughs.

"Just be glad we didn't spend our wedding night there like Aunt Misty and Woody."

My face warms at him mentioning our wedding night, and I stare out the windshield. Our so-called wedding night was spent in separate buildings. Even now, we don't share a room. I'd be lying if I said I hadn't wondered what it would be like to share a room with Liam—including a bed.

But that's not a path I need to travel now.

Liam slows down after a few miles and turns onto a road. At the very end is an RV littered with lights. A giant Santa, even larger than the one on the grocery store, stands in front of it.

"Very festive."

"Speaking of Woody and Misty, that's their place."

I crane my neck to view more decorations in the back as we pass their home. Liam points to an older home on the opposite side of the road.

"That's G-Maw's house."

"Why is her porch green?"

"Oh, that's AstroTurf."

"Like on a football field?"

"Yep, same stuff. G-Maw fell pretty bad when I was in high school. She had some lawn care people who worked on a church soccer field come do her porch."

I turn in my seat to examine it closer as we pass. Every inch is covered in green. I'm decently impressed.

A larger wooden home comes into view. It reminds me of mountain homes on the HGTV vacationing shows. The front porch is the length of the house, and a large dog comes down the steps.

"Don't worry about Bully. He's big but harmless," Liam says as he parks the truck in the front yard.

He opens his door, and the dog howls. Liam pets him while I get out. The dog sniffs me a second, then licks my shirt. I stand petrified at the slobbery tongue mark across my T-shirt.

"Ugh, sorry about that." Liam jerks his collar and pulls him away. "I'll stick him in the pen real quick."

He disappears around the side of the house. I open the back door to get my bags. He will offer to do it for me when he returns, because that's Liam. But I might as well do something instead of stand here.

"Oh, hello!" A loud Southern voice rings out behind me.

I turn my head to two women coming toward me. One is a little older, and the other looks like a younger version of her with longer hair. The younger woman holds on to the porch rail with one hand and a very pregnant belly with the other.

This has to be Liam's mom and sister.

The older lady wraps her arms around me, causing me to drop the duffle bag in my hand. She bends and picks it up, then slings it over her shoulder.

"Sorry about that. You must be Carmela."

"Carmelita."

She waves a hand wildly. "So sorry, honey. Carmelita."

"It's fine." I smile. It's hard not to like her. She could do nothing different and land an award-winning guest role on *Sweet Magnolias*.

"I'm Robin." She extends the hand she was waving.

I shake it. "Nice to meet you."

She turns my hand over in hers and examines the ring. "Your secret's safe with me." She winks.

My stomach swirls. I have no idea exactly what Liam told her about us other than that we got married. A few times I've started to ask him about the phone conversation with her, then stopped. Part of me doesn't want to know the details.

The pregnant woman, who is obviously Lacie, makes it to us. She lets out a long breath and gives me a gentle hug.

"Hi, I'm Carmelita," I say when she steps back.

"Lacie, Liam's sister."

I smile. "He said you were expecting."

She rubs her belly. "Expecting my husband to bring me some tacos soon."

We all laugh a second. Then Robin's face morphs into a snarl. "This crazy girl is craving Enchilada. My poor grandbaby better not come out with high cholesterol."

I laugh again and make a mental note to at least drive by the Enchilada motel place. Just out of curiosity to check if the real deal matches the picture in my head. Not to try the food, or spend a night there with Liam.

"They interrogated you yet?" Liam's voice booms from the other side of the truck.

I look across the seat at him pulling out the rest of our bags. I halfway smile, then grab the bag nearest me. His hand lands on mine, and he smiles widely. "I've got it."

I slide my hand out from under his and try to beat back the mental thoughts of sharing a room with him. Maybe I should drive by the Enchilada motel to clear those thoughts.

Liam circles the truck looking like a pack mule, with bags slung over both arms and in both hands.

"Sure you don't want me to help?"

"I got it," he says.

I carry my one small makeup bag and purse, while he does all the heavy lifting. Mrs. Sanderson holds the door open, and Lacie waddles in first. She's followed by me, then Liam with the bags. He turns sideways and squeezes in the door, then sets them down in a pile.

"Watch the train, son," Mrs. Sanderson says, sliding my duffle from her shoulder.

Liam toes a suitcase closer to the couch, away from a toy train circling a massive Christmas tree. My insides warm as I scan the decorations. It reminds me of our family tree back home. Mama would collect the discarded pearls deemed not good enough for jewelry and allow me to make ornaments out of them. Lola and me would spend hours with hot glue and ribbon, making pearl angels and stars for the tree.

The Sandersons' tree is more painted handprints and wooden popsicle-stick nativities, but it has the same effect. And makes me a little homesick.

This will be the first Christmas I'm away from the island. At least Liam has a nice family to make me feel welcome.

Everyone stops their chitchat when an older man walks into the room. He stops in front of us with his hands in his pockets.

"She doesn't look pregnant."

I think he's talking about Lacie until Liam speaks up.

"She isn't." He wraps his arm around my shoulder.

"Then why in the Sam Hill did you get married without telling me?"

My shoulder quivers like a dog at the vet. Liam tightens his grip around me and stands a little taller, as if initiating a peeing contest with the man who can only be his dad.

Mr. Sanderson stares at him, then says, "I'm going to pick up the hog."

An odd response given the situation, but not coming from this man. Liam tugs me into his side.

"I'm staying here, with my *wife*." He says "wife" in such an assertive tone that it makes me blush.

Mr. Sanderson passes all of us and steps through the open door. He sticks his head back inside and glares at Liam. "We'll talk later."

Liam lifts his chin and sets his jaw. His dad stomps off the porch. Every head turns to watch him leave.

Mrs. Sanderson attempts to shut the door, but a hand slips in. My nerve flare, and Liam curls his fingertips around my shoulder. I'm certain everyone else is expecting Mr. Sanderson just like me.

Instead, a guy a little older than me with a neatly trimmed beard and a Santa hat sticks his head inside. Mrs. Sanderson steps back for him to enter.

"Ho ho ho, who wants tacos?"

# CHAPTER EIGHT

*Liam*

I clinch my jaw and move past my sister with Carmelita snug against my side. Once we're on the front porch, I shut the door, leaving the circus behind.

For now. Daddy will have one of his famous talks with me later.

He could've called me after Mama told him about the marriage and got it over with. But that's not his style. He's an old-school face-to-face confronter. Not only is that more intimidating for me, but he's also had over a week to stew about it. I'll be lucky to make it out alive.

"Sorry about my dad." I sit in a rocking chair.

Carmelita sits in the chair next to mine. "He took it better than my dad probably would."

I laugh. "That sucks."

"We knew marrying like this wouldn't be well accepted."

"Yeah." I sigh and rub my jaw. "I honestly thought my

parents would be more upset later when you split. Guess we've got that to look forward to."

She pulls her legs into her chest and frowns. My shoulders slump, and I regret bringing that up.

"I should've thought more about that part," she says. "Neither of us deserve a divorce on our record."

"We could always get an annulment."

She drops her legs and turns toward me. "Under what grounds?"

I shrug. "I can claim I married you under duress."

"And what's the definition of that word, Mr. Sanderson?"

"You know very well what it is, Mrs. Sanderson."

She licks her lips, and it makes my toes curl. We sit in silence for a second before she speaks.

"I know exactly what that means, but I don't think you do."

"I totally know that word." I balk.

She raises one brow.

"You caused me due stress?"

Her face curves into a smile that turns into a laugh.

"Fine, I don't know what that means, but I do know it's one of the six reasons you can get an annulment in this state."

She laughs even harder, and I laugh with her. We laugh so hard that she ends up bent over toward my chair. I rest my hand on her knee to steady her.

"I threatened you against your better judgment."

"What?" I lift her head to face me.

She scoots back until her head is resting on the arm of my rocker, halfway in my lap. She giggles a little more, then clears her throat.

"That's what duress means. That I threatened you against your better judgement."

I laugh again. "I'd like to see you try."

"Is that a threat?"

Her dark eyes twinkle with a little something extra I haven't seen in them before. It's a mixture of mischief and playfulness. If I didn't know any better, I'd think my wife was flirting with me.

I dip my head closer to hers to gauge her reaction. She doesn't flinch or even blink. Her eyes are fully focused on my face—in particular on my mouth.

My heart races, and I start to sweat behind my ears, despite the cool weather. I lean closer.

This is it. I'm going to kiss her.

I hope she likes it, but either way we're stuck together for the next year. I'll have plenty of time to plan my next move.

I'm hovering within an inch of her face when I hear a truck door slam and a pig squeal. Carmelita slides her head away and sits upright in her chair. I rock back in mine, both mad and embarrassed at the way this went down.

I didn't get to finish making my move. Even worse, I'm left wondering if she's relieved the kiss didn't happen.

"Howdy, you must be the misses."

My cousin Earl Ed puts his hands on his hips and grins. Daddy opens the driver's door and meets him at the front of the truck.

"Earl Ed, we need to unload this thing."

Earl Ed flips a toothpick in his mouth. "She's got a name. Jack said it was Petunia."

Daddy shakes his head. "Fine, help me unload Petunia, please."

I turn to Carmelita. "I better get Bully moved. They'll want to put the hog in that pen."

"Should I go inside?"

The hog squeals louder. We crane our necks to watch as it bangs against the bed of Daddy's truck.

"I'd say that's best."

"Okay." She smiles and goes inside.

I hurry down the steps and nod toward the side of the house. "I'll move Bully out of the pen."

Bully greets me with a wagging tail. I open the fence and rub his head. He follows me out and growls at the squeals coming around the yard.

Earl Ed is shoving the hog by its butt, and it keeps sitting down. Maybe since the yard slopes slightly, he'll have better luck pushing her down the hill.

"Ain't never seen a hog like this one." He stops and wipes his brow with the back of his hand, then smells his hand and winces. "She about tore Uncle Joey's truck bed up, and now she don't want to move."

"Maybe she knows what's coming?"

He glances at the pig and snorts. "Doubtful."

Bully follows me toward the front yard. Waiting at the top of the slope is Daddy, arms crossed. "Let's talk."

I let out a long breath.

"Why are you married?"

"You and Mama frown upon premarital sex?"

"Liam, this is not a joke. Marriage is serious. You promise to love and protect and stand by someone forever. Regardless of the way your aunt lives, the rest of us still honor that."

"Hey, what's wrong with my mama?" Earl Ed calls from down the hill.

"I was talking about Misty. Get the hog settled and quit listening," Daddy yells to the side.

I bite back a laugh. He talks so loudly, I wouldn't doubt the neighbors hearing him either. And that's saying a lot when you live out like we do.

He glares at me for an answer.

"Daddy, I am serious about this. We married so soon because she needed to stay in the US."

"Is that the only reason you married her?" He narrows his eyes.

*No, I also didn't want to ask you for a boatload of money.*

"No, I really care about her."

That's not the first answer that came to mind, but it's not a lie either. I do care about her. I've always cared about Carmelita, and in the last few weeks, it's led to something deeper.

"I love her."

My tongue stings when the words leave my mouth. Yes, I'm trying to get Daddy off my back. However, saying it out loud freed up a lot of tension I didn't realize I had. My shoulders relax and my stomach unknots. The cat's out of the bag, as G-Maw says. I can rest now that I've admitted how I truly feel.

Just not to her—yet.

Daddy's scowl softens a bit. "Just remember there are only three things in life meant to be permanent—your salvation, your teeth, and your marriage."

"Good talk." I nod, then pat him on the shoulder.

One thing I've learned in my past twenty-two years is to get out while he's in a good mood. I start up the porch, relieved to see him headed toward the pen out the corner of my eye.

Earl Ed can deal with his lectures for a while.

My stomach twists when I open the front door. The house is warm and smells like a mixture of Mama's Christmas candles and Enchilada. A perfect combo to make me queasy. I need to lie down on the couch, but first I need to find my wife.

Yes, my wife. Maybe not for life, but I'll cross that bridge when I get there. Besides, I have a paper napkin wadded up in my gun safe as evidence she agreed to stay with me for a year. A lot can happen in a year, including Carmelita loving me.

I head toward voices in the hallway and stop at my sister's old room. Carmelita sits on the edge of the bed, looking toward the closet. I slide inside the room.

"And we have more blankets up here in case you get cold."

Mama has her head in Lacie's old closet.

"You doing okay?" I ask.

Carmelita notices me by the door and grins. "Yes. Your mom has been so nice. We've eaten fudge, and she's showing me where everything is."

"Okay." I scan the room. "Wait, where's Lacie and Collins sleeping?"

Mama steps away from the closet with an armful of patch blankets G-Maw and Aunt Bea made like a million years ago.

"They claimed the basement when they got here. Lacie said it's good for her to walk stairs every day to keep her blood circulating." Her voice turns to a whisper. "But I think she really wants to be down there with the snack bar and mini fridge so she can eat a bunch of junk without me judging."

My eyes widen. "Collins is okay with that?" I turn to Carmelita. "Since he's a doctor and all."

She nods.

Mama laughs, then continues whispering. "I think he likes eating it too." She snarls. "Except Enchilada. Your sister's the only one who can seem to stomach that."

I step toward the wall and bump into my suitcase and duffle bag.

"I'll get these out of the way." I bend and pick them up.

"Where are you going?"

I lift my head to Carmelita. "My room. It's right beside here if you need anything."

"Nonsense." Mama swats a hand my way. "You kids are married. You can stay right here."

I scrunch my face in confusion. Mama crosses the room and takes a bag from my hand. "It doesn't matter how you kids got married—you're married."

My neck heats up. I'm not sure I like discussing such things with my mama. It gets even more awkward when she steps closer to me and whispers, "We don't need any more reasons for Joey to question the validity of this marriage, do we?"

I cut my eyes toward Carmelita. Her lips are pressed together and she shrugs. I let the duffle bag hit the floor.

Mama pats my face and leaves the room. I sit on the edge of Lacie's old bed. I turn to Carmelita and sigh. "Looks like you're stuck with me this week."

"For better or worse." She smiles when I frown. "Just kidding—kind of."

I plop my head back on the bed and pull my cap over my eyes. It's going to be an interesting week.

*Carmelita*

With Liam's eyes securely covered by his cap so he can't see me, I study him.

His chest rises and falls as he breathes slowly. He's within an inch of me, and it's the closest we've come all day besides the incident on the porch.

Incident sounds like something in a crime report.

Encounter maybe? No, that sounds like something offered at a petting zoo. I'll go with moment.

In that moment, Liam almost kissed me. At least, I think he did. Loud noises startled me, and I pulled away before he could. And like that, the moment passed.

I regret not letting things play out, but I didn't want to kiss him for the first time in front of an audience. Of course, any other married couple would've kissed many times before. Too bad our marriage isn't typical.

I breathe in his clean scent that's mixed with something a little earthy. Most likely a little hint of the dog and hog outside. I smile to myself, then tiptoe toward the edge of the room to grab some of my things.

Sitting next to Liam on the bed conjures up unexpected emotions I'm not ready to tackle. What I can tackle is my dirty hair.

Mrs. Sanderson gave me a thorough tour of the house, including all the items I'd need in the bathroom. I slide into the hallway and shut the bedroom door behind me so Liam can rest. The bathroom is down the hall, with the door cracked.

I open it wider and hear a hurling sound. I peek my head around the corner to Lacie on all fours in front of the toilet. As I'm backing away, she stands and flushes the toilet. She spots me before I can leave.

"Oh hey, Carmelita. I'm finished in here." She sticks out her tongue and winces. "Ugh, Enchilada hit extra hard today." She grabs a washcloth and walks toward the door. "It's all yours. I better head downstairs and brush my teeth."

I watch in silence as she waddles down the hallway, wiping her tongue with the hand towel. Then I step in the bathroom and lock the door.

I run a cloth over my face under the warm shower

stream. I empathize with Lacie wiping her mouth. It must suck to have odd cravings and get sick at random times.

Pregnancy is something I've never considered. Probably because kids are something I haven't thought about in a long time. I like kids and always assumed I'd have my own one day. I don't have a ton of experience with them, being an only child, but I get along with them well.

I finish my shower and try to dismiss the thought of kids. I have plenty of time to worry about starting a family after I settle down. After Liam.

My hands shake as I pull on my clothes. It bothers me to think of life after Liam, and I can't explain why.

I flip my hair and blast hot air across it. The hair dryer buzzes near my ear, bringing my mind back to the present. I have no idea how this year of my life will play out.

My immediate concern is this week—starting with tonight. I'm about to eat dinner with all of the Sandersons, including the man who said I didn't look pregnant. I guess I should be flattered, but I doubt he meant it as a compliment.

I brush my hair and pull it back to apply my makeup. A few minutes later, I have a fresh face. I go down the hall with my bags and find the bedroom door open. Liam isn't on the bed either.

"Hey."

I step back to Liam peeking from his room. My stomach buckles. Is he moving in there?

"Thanks for letting me rest."

"Of course."

He disappears, then passes me with a pillow. I watch him toss it on the bed.

"Don't worry. I'll move it to the floor when it's time to sleep."

I curve my lips in a slight smile. So he *is* staying in this room with me. My stomach takes on a new form of nervousness.

"Mama said whenever you're ready we can eat."

I drop my bags on the floor. "Oh gosh, you didn't have to wait on me."

"It's not a big deal. Daddy prefers to eat later, and Lacie's been ready for dinner since barfing up her afternoon snack."

I wrinkle my nose and he laughs.

"Sorry for the visual."

"It's fine." I try and erase the actual memory of her doing so.

I follow Liam toward the kitchen, where Mrs. Sanderson is moving candy away from Lacie. "Now, that's enough. You need to eat supper first."

"Mama, I'm twenty-seven and about to be a mama myself."

"Then you should know better." She picks up a wooden spoon and points it at Collins. "And so should you." Then she stirs something in a pot on the stove.

Lacie pouts until she sees us. "Hey, Liam and Carmelita are here. We can eat!"

Mrs. Sanderson shakes her head and opens a cabinet above her.

"I've got it." Liam reaches up and takes down bowls.

"Thank you, son."

Lacie snorts. "You should've gotten married a long time ago if that's what's making you help."

"Lacie." Her mom scowls. "Mind your manners." She points the spoon at her this time. "And don't use hormones as an excuse. Just wait until you hit menopause."

"Eww," Lacie groans.

"She's right," Collins says.

Liam unstacks the bowls on the counter, while his mom

takes a pan of bread from the oven. My stomach rumbles when the scent of baked corn hits the air.

"Go ahead and fix your plates, kids. I'll get your daddy."

Lacie races toward the bowls when her mom leaves the kitchen. Liam holds his hands up when she bumps into him.

"Slow down. You do know babies only weigh like twenty pounds. The rest of all that will stick to you."

Lacie slaps his arm, and he laughs.

"Actually, babies weigh more like six to eight pounds on average," Collins corrects.

Lacie and Liam glare at him.

"What?"

I pour vegetable soup into a bowl as Lacie slices the cornbread. She pulls a huge piece for herself and sets it on a plate. By the time the rest of us fix our plates and pour drinks, Liam's parents are back in the kitchen.

"Smells great, honey," Mr. Sanderson says.

I take the seat next to Liam and meet his gaze. He sets his hand on my knee under the table and gives it a gentle squeeze. I relax against the wooden chair and listen as Mr. Sanderson says a prayer.

He's acting calm and everyone is focused more on their meal than me. That's a huge relief. Lacie finishes eating before everyone else, then brings the plate of candy to the kitchen table.

My eyes widen. There's even more than this afternoon.

"What is all this?"

Mrs. Sanderson beams. "Haystacks, another flavor of fudge, and some chocolate-covered peanut candy."

"Sounds delicious."

"Thank you, Carmelita. Help yourself."

I select one of the chocolate peanut candies and take a bite. I swallow and lick my lips. "This is amazing."

Mrs. Sanderson sits up straighter and smiles wider.

"Let me try." Liam bends toward me and bites off the piece in my hand.

My fingers twitch as his lips brush them. Sharing the same piece of candy wouldn't be uncommon for a married couple—unless it's us.

I'm certain he either did it out of impulse to try the treat or to sell our marriage to his parents. Regardless, it was more intimate than any other encounter—rather "moment"—we've had . . . including the almost kiss on the front porch.

His lips touched me for the first time.

The rest of the meal is a blur. I manage to finish my tea and eat another piece of candy, but my brain is locked on analyzing Liam's behavior.

Even after dinner, he's extra attentive to me. We move to the living room, where Lacie puts on *Elf*. At first I justify his squishing beside me on the couch to make room for Collins. But he wraps his arm around me and relaxes against me. Before the movie ends, I rest my head against his shoulder.

That's the last thing I remember until I blink open my eyes to a dark room. I'm in the bed, still wearing my sweatshirt and jeans. My shoes are off, and the only light is glowing plastic stars on the ceiling.

"Lacie N Co?"

"Used to say 'Collins,' I think."

I sit up and reach for the bedside lamp. Liam shades his eyes when I turn it on. He's lying on the floor on some of the extra quilts Mrs. Sanderson took from the closet.

"What time is it?" I ask.

He blinks and sits up, the cover sliding down his bare chest.

"Uh, like eleven, maybe? You fell asleep during *Elf*, so I brought you in here. I only took off your shoes."

I glance down at my jeans. "Thanks."

"I'll lie back down if you want to change. Don't worry,

the door is locked, but you can use the bathroom if it makes you feel more comfortable."

My cheeks warm at his concern. "I totally trust you. Ever since we've been . . ." My voice trails, as I'm not certain what to call this. "You've slept on the floor and been a gentleman."

"Thanks. I even slept in shorts for you." He grins sleepily and throws the cover off his legs to reveal gym shorts.

I laugh. "What do you usually sleep in?" My entire face heats at the flirty tone of my voice. It wasn't intentional.

"Boxers." He shrugs. "Anyway, I'm going back to sleep. Feel free to do whatever except steal my pillow."

He beds down and covers his face. I stare at him a second before grabbing a pair of pajamas and changing on the other end of the room. Then I climb in bed and turn out the light.

It takes me a while to go back to sleep. Not because of the stupid stars, but because Liam's a few feet away from me, and I'm not sure if I want him farther or closer.

# CHAPTER NINE

*Liam*

I roll over and yawn, then stretch my back. If I weren't so set on proving to Daddy that my marriage is for real, I'd have moved to the couch hours ago.

Carmelita is nowhere in the room, and the bed is made. If the old clock on the wall is right, I'm probably the last to wake up. Typical. When I don't have class or work, I either wake before the sun to go hunting or sleep extra late to catch up on sleep lost hunting.

I get dressed and hear voices when I open the door. I don't want to leave Carmelita in there to fend for herself, but take a few minutes to comb my hair and run a razor across my face after I brush my teeth. I also don't want her to think I'm a slob.

*What does Carmelita think of me?* That's the million-dollar question. I have no idea what she thinks about my personality or my looks. All more the reason to keep my hair combed.

I whistle on my way out of the bathroom, trying to act confident instead of nervous. Never before have I had to win over a girl I'm already in a relationship with, but there's a first time for everything—like getting married.

Bacon fills the air when I'm halfway down the hall. I sigh and take a big whiff. Everyone is in the kitchen, with Carmelita sitting next to my sister. I stop and fix a plate of what's left, which isn't much.

"Morning, son. I made Lacie save a piece of bacon for you."

"Thanks, Mama." I scowl at my sister, who shrugs.

I'll be glad when this baby pops out and she goes back to eating like a girl instead of a pro lumberjack. After pouring a glass of milk, I pull a stool to the table and sit beside Carmelita.

Daddy watches us over his morning paper. I smile at her. "Good morning, beautiful."

She smiles back.

Daddy's eyes narrow on me, so I give her a quick kiss on the cheek. She continues smiling, although it may be for sake of playing along. "Sleep well?" she asks.

"I did," I lie.

She nods and sips her coffee. That little charade is enough to shift Daddy's glare back to the sports section. I sigh and bite into my one measly piece of bacon.

"What are y'all's plans for today?" Mama asks.

I glance at Carmelita, then Mama.

"Whatever she wants to do. I could show her around our land, take her hunting—"

Lacie lets out an annoying cackle.

"What?"

"Hunting, really? If you want her to see Apple Cart County, take her to the cow-patty drop."

"The what?" Carmelita wrinkles her forehead.

"It's a fundraiser for the Angel Tree. They buy gifts for needy kids." Mama continues overexplaining the purpose of the Angel Tree until Daddy sets down his paper and interrupts.

"You bet on where a cow poops on the football field."

Carmelita blinks. "Oh."

"It sounds gross and all, but it's actually entertaining." Collins grins, then forms a small circle with his hands. "Their aunt makes these cow-butt cookies and they taste phenomenal." He chuckles. "There's even these little chocolate drops like the poop."

Daddy frowns at Collins, and he stops laughing.

"Anyways . . ." Lacie smiles at Carmelita. "We're about to head that way if y'all want to ride with us."

"Now, that's exciting," Mama adds. "My two kids and their significant others bonding."

Lacie stands and rubs her big belly. "Let's go ahead and go before all the cookies are gone."

Carmelita drinks the last sip of her coffee and smiles at me.

"I'll get the van." Collins stands and starts clearing his and Lacie's plates.

She reaches for half a cinnamon roll left on top as he takes them to the sink. Carmelita and I share a look before standing and taking our own plates. Lacie smacks the cinnamon roll as we go to the garage.

"Y'all are going to love the new van." She licks her fingers. "It's loaded. Watch this." She hurries in front of us and pushes a button on the door.

All the doors slide open. Lacie stares at us with wide eyes.

"Uh, yeah, that's sweet," I say.

We climb in the back, and Lacie hits the button again. The doors shut. She rubs her hands together, then presses more buttons, explaining what each one does.

I smirk at Carmelita. She bites back a laugh.

Lacie may think her van is the best ever, but I'd rather be in any ride right now that doesn't have bucket seats. Carmelita feels a million miles away.

I'm jerked back to the reality of why I'm in this van when Collins hits a pothole.

"Sorry, just making sure y'all are awake back there." He smiles back at us and hits another one.

"Babe, watch out." Lacie finally stops fumbling with controls and braces her hands on the dash.

Collins slows to a crawl and maneuvers around one more crater before parking. Lacie practically rolls out the front. I'm still not used to seeing her walk around like she's got a watermelon under her shirt.

Both back doors slide open, and Carmelita and I exit. She cranes her neck and surveys the parking lot and buildings. "You went to school here?"

"Yep, and my love of big trucks started with having to drive through this parking lot." I kick at the edge of a pothole.

"I get it now."

I nod and reach for her hand. She allows me to take it and laces her fingers with mine. We follow Lacie and Collins to the football field, gaining a few stares from onlookers. Their eyes reveal a layer of nosiness, itching to find out more about the pretty dark-haired girl by my side. I stand a little taller, gloating at giving them all something new to worry about.

The last time I was the talk of the town, I attempted to spray paint the water tower with two of my buddies.

Kyle stands near the entrance to the bleachers with a clipboard in hand. Collins smiles and picks up the pace. He leads us straight to Kyle and pulls out his wallet. "I want to put five on every square."

Kyle's eyes widen. "While the Apple Cart County Tractor Pull Association appreciates your generous donation, we can't have multiple bids on the same square. You can only purchase blank spaces."

Collins nods and sighs. "Okay, put me down for what you can."

Kyle hands him back some cash and starts writing on his board. An older couple comes up and asks about a space. He lifts his head. "Sorry, we're sold out."

"Sold out?" The man's mouth drops. "Y'all ain't sold out this fast in twenty years."

"Sir, this is only the third year."

The man squints at Kyle, then his wife. She shakes her head and leads him away.

Kyle finishes marking off large areas with Collins's name, then closes his clipboard. "Good luck. We start in a few minutes."

Carmelita cocks her head. "How long does this usually last?"

"Why, are you bored? Should we go hunting instead?" I wink.

She frowns, and Lacie swats my arm. "We haven't even gotten a cookie yet, or gone ice skating."

"Lacie, I think you've had enough candy already."

She pops me harder.

"Ouch." I rub my arm. "I don't think you should be ice skating in your condition. Besides, I'm not allowed to skate here."

"Why, did Mama ground you?" She grins mischievously.

"No, for your information, a missing skate was found in my room a few years back and I'm now banned."

"I knew it was you!" Collins points at my chest.

"Whatever, I'm getting one of Aunt Carla's cookies." Lacie marches toward the side of the field, and we follow. Carmelita has held my hand so long, she feels like a natural extension of me.

Sadly, she's forced to break our bond when Aunt Carla squeezes her in a giant hug. Carmelita drops my hand to pat her back, then wiggle herself loose.

"I can't believe Liam is married!" Aunt Carla claps and bounces on her toes.

Several people turn their heads when she yells. I see one woman mouth "married?" to another. My neck heats up.

"I was going to wait and surprise everyone with the news at G-Maw's." I try and act casual.

Aunt Carla fans a hand and laughs. "Crazy, boy. Everyone in town knows."

"They do?"

"Of course. Woody couldn't wait to spread the word soon as he ran into y'all at that modular home show."

I find Carmelita's hand again and give it a squeeze. She raises her brow, as if sensing my tension. I loosen my grip to not cut off her circulation.

"And G-Maw?" I ask.

Despite the mild weather, sweat beads on my forehead. The one person I don't want hearing about my life from anyone but me is my grandmother. She's a big gossiper and a little forgetful at times. Whatever she hears first, she believes to be the gospel about anything. No matter if it comes straight from the source or from a random person in line at the Piggly Wiggly checkout. Or God forbid, the hair salon.

She has a standing appointment every week. If she's been to get her hair set since Woody saw us, it's too late.

"She's at home getting everything ready for the week's events."

I shake my head. "I meant . . ." I shake my head again. "Never mind. Aunt Carla, we'll have to catch up in a bit."

I lead Carmelita toward the ice skating rink, where box fans blare an awful noise. She winces at the sound.

"We need to go see my grandma ASAP."

"Did you say we need to bring a mouse trap?"

I sigh and put my mouth to her ear. "We need to see my grandma as soon as possible."

My lips brush the lobe of her ear, sending a jolt of electricity down my spine. Who would've thought whispering the word "grandma" could turn me on?

*Carmelita*

A bright blue truck even larger than Liam's pulls up to the parking lot. The window rolls down, revealing Earl Ed.

"Y'all ready?"

Liam opens the back door, then rests his hand on my back as I climb in. He's given me a lot of touches and attention today. I'm sure it's to make our relationship believable, but I'm not complaining.

Even in the middle of nowhere, among people I've never met, I've never felt so comfortable. That's because of Liam. And for the moment, also because of this luxury truck with heated back seats.

"Thanks, Earl Ed. What do I owe you?" Liam asks.

He laughs loudly. "I ain't letting you pay me to drive you to G-Maw's."

"I called you for an Uber ride."

"I'll let G-Maw pay me in food."

"Thanks, man."

Earl Ed looks at me, then back at Liam before turning toward the road to drive.

"What made y'all decide to get married?"

*Well that escalated quickly.* I suck in a deep breath, and Liam reaches for my hand. His touch calms me as much as anything could, but the question still makes my skin itch with nerves.

"We've known each other a few years in college. I just never talked about her to y'all, because I always thought she was out of my league." He gives my hand a squeeze.

I glance over, and he smiles at me. Either Liam is really quick-witted with answers, or there's some truth to that statement. If it's the latter, I'm both flattered and sad—flattered to think he considered dating me before, but sad he thought I wouldn't date him.

Not that I sent out vibes of wanting to date. My time was split between school and work, and had been since the moment I landed in Alabama. I've been so busy avoiding a relationship with Antonio that I've avoided a relationship with anyone.

"I get that," Earl Ed says. "I still don't get what Mackenzie sees in me half the time."

"Is she coming down this week?" Liam asks.

"Yeah, she's finishing up something for work first."

Liam turns to me. "His girlfriend is a director. They met last year when she did a show about Aunt Carla's cookies."

"The cow cookies?"

"Those and others." Earl Ed laughs. "Just wait until you see her reindeer in an ugly sweater or the camouflage snowman. That's my personal favorite."

I laugh. "They all sound so cute."

"And delicious," Liam adds.

Earl Ed nods in agreement as he slows to turn onto their road. We pull up to G-Maw's house, and I get a close-up view of her AstroTurf.

When we open our doors, Woody's giant Santa belts out, "Ho, ho, ho, Merry Christmas!"

"Well, that's new," Liam comments.

"Yeah, Woody said Mama's decorations inspired him to add sound this year. I think he's also noticed he's run himself out of yard."

"True." Liam shakes his head at the large display of blow-up and plastic figurines.

"He's the first person I've known to make flamingos look like reindeer, and I grew up on a tropical island."

The guys laugh at my comment.

"He does have an eye for that sort of thing." Earl Ed smiles admiringly at the display across the road. "If I didn't want to keep from totally embarrassing our family, I'd tell Mackenzie to get him on one of those holiday light-fight shows."

Liam and I laugh as we follow Earl Ed up G-Maw's porch. He knocks on the door. After a minute, he knocks louder. The door opens to a woman even smaller than me. She sticks her hand out and motions us inside.

"Come on in, kids. I made breakfast for lunch."

"You mean brunch?" Earl Ed asks.

"You know your G-Paw thinks that word is silly."

When I step inside, G-Maw grabs my cheek and pats it. "Oh, you're beautiful. I can't believe Liam has hid you from me this long."

"Thanks."

I blush at the idea of tricking a sweet old lady. Even though we're married, it's under false pretenses I hope she never hears about.

G-Maw slides her hand away from my cheek and loops

her arm through mine. She shuffles slowly past the living room, and I slow to match her steps. We stop at the kitchen.

An older man, who is obviously G-Paw, sits at the end of the table running a long knife across a sharpening block. Under any other circumstances, this scene would freak me out.

"Ed, move your knife so we can eat, please."

"You made me peas?" G-Paw yells at G-Maw.

Poor man, he wouldn't have a chance at hearing anyone near the ice skating rink.

G-Maw scoots closer to him and leans down. "It's time to eat."

"Kill the beef?" He taps the knife. "I'm getting ready for it."

G-Maw pats his shoulder and shuffles toward the sink. She lifts a large iron bell from the windowsill. Earl Ed and Liam cover their ears as she rings it wildly.

"Dinnertime!" G-Paw grins. He stands and places his knife and sharpener on a nearby countertop.

G-Maw brings a pan of biscuits to the table. Earl Ed and Liam silently grab dishes and set them where she directs like they've done this a million times. Nostalgia, mixed with a hint of jealousy, hits me. I swallow back the emotions of not being in my parents' kitchen this Christmas with my lola.

"Liam, will you go downstairs and grab more orange juice?"

"Yes, ma'am."

"I'll help you," I offer.

Everyone stares at me with jaws dropped. I blink.

"You don't want to go down there," Earl Ed whispers.

"Why not?"

"The pig," he answers, still whispering.

"Mr. Sanderson's hog?"

G-Maw laughs. "No, honey. Earl Ed is terrified of a dead

pig in the basement."

He shudders, and Liam laughs.

"Did you already kill a hog this week?"

"No, it's a pickled pig in a jar," Liam answers.

"Pig's feet?"

"No, come on." He stands and takes my hand.

He leads me to the back of the house and down a flight of wooden steps into a cold basement. He flips a light on, and I scan the area.

There's a dirt floor, several freezers and refrigerators, and shelves of canned food. Liam slides behind one of the freezers and holds up a large jar. A tiny smooshed pig face stares at me.

"Of all the things I've seen served in mason jars at farmers' markets, this is new."

Liam laughs. "It's not to eat. It was Aunt Misty's science project. She was supposed to dissect this for biology, but quit college first. G-Paw keeps it here out of stubbornness."

"Isn't Misty like fifty?" I wrinkle my nose at the weird object.

"Yep, so this thing's been here a while. But she went back to hair school, so maybe it will resurface soon." He frowns at the jar, then sets it in the corner of the room.

I open the closest refrigerator in search of orange juice. My eyes widen. "I've never seen this many pickles in one place, including the grocery store."

Liam nods and pulls a jar of something gooey from the door. I'm afraid to ask what it is.

"This is her garden fridge. Drinks are in the middle."

I move to that one and grab a bottle of orange juice. "Why is there so much sweet tea in here?"

He laughs. "That must be left over from Thanksgiving. G-Maw's tea is so strong, Mama brings reserves for family gatherings." He shuts the refrigerator door and holds a hand out. "I can carry that for you." He reaches for the jug. When his hands brush mine, I grip it tighter instead of letting go.

"Thanks for making me feel welcome here. I was nervous about coming, but it's been comfortable, normal, like we're really married."

He steps closer, so the only thing between us is the bottle of orange juice. Our eyes lock and he smiles before whispering, "Carmelita, we are really married."

My heart beats in my throat, and I let out a nervous squeak. He dips his head and licks his lips. My hands tingle to the point of numbness. *Is he about to kiss me?*

If he is, what would that mean? There's not anyone here to see it. Unless you count the pickled pig in the corner, which I don't.

Liam tilts his head slightly, and I suck in a breath. Yep, he's going to kiss me. I close my eyes and try to calm my nerves.

His lips brush against mine for a millisecond before a loud gong rings above our heads. It startles me, and I jump, letting go of the jug.

Glass shatters at our feet, and orange juice soaks into the dirt. Liam bends down and touches my foot. "Are you okay? Did any glass get on you?"

"Uh, I don't think so."

I'm still in shock from the kiss and the bell, which is ringing again. Liam hurries to the stairs and yells up them, "Be there in a minute! Hold on!"

He rushes back and opens the refrigerator for more juice. "Take this to them so G-Paw will start eating and quit ringing that bell. I'll clean up the glass, then be up shortly."

My mouth twitches into a slight smile. I take the new glass jug and nod. Then I walk carefully upstairs, trying to ignore the third bell ring . . .

And the fact that Liam kissed me—in private.

## CHAPTER TEN

*Liam*

When I return to the kitchen, G-Maw is grilling Carmelita about what brought her to Auburn and how she grew up. Poor Carmelita barely has time to swallow a bite between answering her questions about everything from what they eat for holidays to if they have a Piggly Wiggly on her island.

She names off some of the delicious foods she's cooked for us, then says "no" about the Pig.

"That's a shame. They really do have the best quality meat." G-Maw sips her own tea and smiles. "Except for all meat we kill, cut, and cook ourselves."

Earl Ed grunts and shakes his head. I glance at him and smirk. He may own a mini-golf and go-kart place with a deep-fry grill, but he can cook any high-end food imaginable. He's the food snob of the family, and G-Maw often complains that he doesn't give soul food enough credit.

I slide in the seat beside Carmelita and fill my plate with

a biscuit and gravy. There isn't any bacon left, which is fitting given this morning. Unlike Mama, G-Maw is old school. If you're not there when the prayer is prayed, no food will get saved. The bell rang so many times, I doubt Carmelita got any bacon either.

But she may not want any after coming face to face with Aunt Misty's pig.

I pay attention to all Carmelita's answers, since G-Maw asks questions that never would've crossed my mind. Like what's the main language of her island. It's English, but that's still a smart question. She also asks if they have any pets at her home or a garden on their property. G-Maw would've made a great reporter, especially for the *Apple Cart Weekly*, since it's a hodgepodge of weather, event announcements, and town gossip.

*No pets, no garden except for flowers. They do have a swimming pool.* I file this away in the part of my brain I've committed to facts about Carmelita. It's growing by the minute. If only I could major in her instead of engineering. Talk about an easy A.

"Where are y'all headed when you leave here?" G-Maw asks.

"Who shot a deer?" G-Paw asks loudly.

"Nobody," Earl Ed and I answer together.

Satisfied with that answer, which is true, G-Paw nods and focuses his attention on his food. G-Maw reaches over and twists his hearing aid. It beeps, and he winces.

"We're heading back to Mama's," I say to G-Maw.

"If you don't mind, could one of you drop off my Angel Tree gifts? I don't feel like getting dressed to go into town today."

I blink. G-Maw is dressed like always except for wearing her house slippers. She's the only person I know who dresses for church every day, when she sits at home ninety percent of the time.

Lacie gave her more casual clothes once, and she refused to wear them. Her reasoning is that if she's ever caught dead anywhere other than in her sleep, she needs to look nice. Maybe I'll care more when I get close to eighty. Right now there's a good chance the coroner will be cutting me out of camo.

"We can run them by," I say.

"Thanks, man. I need to check all the lights before tonight," Earl Ed says.

"What's tonight?" Carmelita asks.

"Double Drive is closed as of today for Christmas, but I light up the entire golf course and let people pay to walk through and see the lights."

"It's pretty cool. We can check it out if you want," I say to her.

"Sounds like fun."

"It's way better quality than Woody's," I add.

"Now, Woody put a lot of work into his place," G-Maw says. "I just wish he'd turn it off every once in a while so we could sleep."

"If I wanted to live in lights, I'd move to town," G-Paw adds.

Carmelita grins at me. My eyes drop to her lips, and my stomach churns. If that dang bell hadn't scared her, I could've finished the kiss. Now I'm back to the awkwardness of working up my courage to kiss her again.

Maybe tonight after I show her the lights. I don't want to wait until we're in my room. That might suggest that I'm looking for more than a kiss.

*She is your legal wife.*

My mind drifts to places I don't need it to. Then a bag of

diapers falls in my lap. If this is a sign from God to behave, message received.

"Sorry, Liam. That slipped."

G-Maw stands beside me with an armload of gifts. Earl Ed gets up and takes some from her. I reach up and take what's left.

"Thank you, boys. I'll get the rest."

We exchange a look. How much more can there be?

That question is answered when Carmelita and I are squished together in the back of Earl Ed's truck by everything G-Maw insisted would blow away in the bed. I almost reminded her Mama's house is just down the road, but decided to let it go.

Any excuse to sit next to Carmelita and work up the courage to steal another kiss is great with me.

*Carmelita*

Liam's truck is packed to the roof. I'm sandwiched between the door and a box of stuffed animals, with a pile of clothes in my lap.

He promised G-Maw he wouldn't put anything in the bed of the truck, and he didn't. That's sweet of him, even if I'm a bit claustrophobic at the moment.

"Thanks for hanging in there and holding that stuff."

I turn to answer him, but come face to face with a stuffed bear. "No problem."

"I never could lie to G-Maw, even about little things."

"That's a good thing."

# QUEEN OF MY DOUBLE-WIDE TRAILER

Liam turns onto the main road. Luckily there's no traffic, as I doubt he has a peripheral view. He turns beside the Dollar General store, down a road I hadn't noticed before. A tall building pops up out of nowhere with a sign that reads, "Wisteria City Hall."

Multiple cars line the parking lot. Liam finds a place close to the building. I open my door and wiggle to turn my feet without dropping any clothes. Before I can feel for the running board, Liam is at my side. He puts his hands on my waist and sets me on the ground. It's all I can do not to drop the pile of clothes separating us.

The quick kiss in G-Maw's basement rattled me. Ever since, I've wanted to ask him about it. Why did he kiss me—with nobody around?

Although we drove here alone, I couldn't even see him over all the stuff in the truck. I need to see his reaction when I bring up the kiss.

"Let me get that," Liam says. He slides his hands away from my waist, sending a jolt of electricity with them. Then he takes the clothes in his arms.

"Actually, I'll get that, big dog." A guy in a uniform and cowboy hat stands behind Liam with his arms wide.

Liam balances the clothes to one side and holds out his hand. The guy takes it and pulls him in for a side hug. A few shirts fall from the top of the stack. I bend and pick them up.

"I'll take that," the officer says.

I read "Sheriff Bradley Manning" on his badge as I hand him the clothes. Unless there's a new sheriff in town, this has to be the guy Lacie once dated.

He makes eye contact with me and nods. "Howdy, ma'am. Welcome to Apple Cart County."

Liam opens the back door and more things fall to the ground. I hurry to help him pick them up.

"Good night, is this from Robin?" Bradley asks.

"G-Maw," Liam answers.

"Hold up, let me get the sled." He disappears around the corner, carrying the clothes.

Liam and I stack boxes and straighten the loose items.

"G-Maw has both a generous heart and an addiction to Dollar General."

"I can tell." I laugh.

Something beeps beside us, and Liam turns his head. I follow his gaze to a small cab with a large inclined bed decorated with Christmas garland.

"That's not the sled I imagined," Liam says.

"What is that?"

"It's the literal sled for the tractor pull, but my guess is they're trying to pass it off as Santa's sleigh."

"Tractor pull?"

Liam smirks. "That's in the summer. Don't worry, you have plenty of time to learn all about it. And yes, it's about as boring as it sounds."

Bradley hops out of the cab and grabs a few boxes from our pile. Liam and I exchange a look, then follow him with more boxes. Behind the decorative red sides is a long black platform. He sets the gifts on top, and they slide to the bottom like a conveyor belt.

"Hey, you two should help me deliver these."

Liam seethes, and I'm afraid to ask why.

Bradley slaps him on the shoulder. "Don't worry, big dog. The lead role is already covered. I just need some muscle to help unload the sleigh."

Liam looks to me as if asking my opinion. I have no idea where we're going, but delivering presents has to rank above hunting or waiting on a cow to poop.

"Sure?" I say with a hint of hesitation in my voice.

"That's the spirit." Bradley pats my head like I'm a puppy. "Lock up your truck and come on."

We do as he says and meet him back at the sled. Liam opens the back door, and we climb inside. There's a small seat next to the driver's. Liam sits down and pats his knee. I sit in his lap and try to act like this isn't the first time I've done so.

This would make a great time to talk about our kiss. Except for the sheriff sitting beside us whistling "Christmas in Dixie." The fact that I recognize such a song so easily proves I belong in Alabama rather than Oval Island.

"I thought the belts were exposed on this thing?" Liam asks. His breath tickles my ear, sending chill bumps down my neck.

"I had Kyle build a cover, then Daisy and Carolina designed the sides to make it look all festive." Bradley smiles at us. "It was all my idea."

"Of course." Liam turns to me and smirks.

Our faces are inches apart, which turns my chill bumps into heat bumps. If that's even a thing. Would he kiss me again if Bradley weren't here?

That thought hits the back burner when we hit a dirt road. I bounce on Liam's lap, and he holds on to my waist to steady me. I lean against him and rest the back of my head on his shoulder. His arms wrap around my waist in the most natural way.

Bradley comes to an abrupt stop, ending our comfy embrace.

"All right, elves." He bends down and pulls out two pair of headbands with elf ears.

"No," Liam says when Bradley holds out a pair for him.

I laugh and put a pair on. Liam frowns at me, then the pair in Bradley's hand. He sighs and snatches the ears, then shoves them on his head. Bradley leans down again and grabs a Santa suit before opening the door.

Once we're all on the ground, he steps into the suit and covers his face with a fake beard. Then he fits a Santa hat over the top of his cowboy hat. Liam and I exchange a look, and he hides a laugh.

Bradley claps his hands together. "Ho, ho, ho, helpers. We're ready for the kids."

Liam shrugs, and we follow Bradley around the front of the barn and toward the farmhouse at the end of the drive. We pass a large cedar tree covered with lights in the front yard. Bradley knocks loudly on the front door. Liam and I stay back on the porch steps like a pair of clueless puppies following their pack leader.

The door opens to an attractive woman with a toddler hugging her legs. Her eyes are kind, but tired. She smiles and opens the door wider before calling behind her, "Kids, you have a visitor."

Kids ranging in age from the one clinging to her side to teenagers come to the door. Every face lights up when they see Bradley. Even the tallest boy takes out his earbuds and smiles.

"Ho, ho, howdy, little buddies. Santa's got a sled full of toys for y'all!"

Some of the kids jump, and one girl screams. My heart swells with their excitement. The second Bradley turns around, the kids push past their mom and rush after him. One of the older kids picks up the toddler and takes her with them.

"It's so great of y'all to come do this every year," the woman says.

"Thanks." I try and sound like I didn't just join in at the last minute.

"Y'all come in, it's getting cool."

Liam and I climb the porch and follow her inside.

"I'm Lina, by the way. This is my husband, Andy."

"Hi." Andy raises a hand.

"Liam." They shake hands.

"I'm Carmelita." I shake his hand as well, then notice a young boy sitting near the fireplace.

"Why isn't he outside with everyone?"

Lina frowns. "That's Pablo. He probably didn't understand. We only started fostering him last month, and he barely speaks any English."

I wrinkle my forehead and study his cute, chubby face as he runs a toy truck across the floor. I turn to Lina. "He speaks Spanish?"

She nods.

I remove the oversized elf ears before inching toward him. I bend down and tell him my name. When he looks up, I smile. My Spanish is a little rusty, but I string enough words together to ask him what he wants for Christmas.

He grins, holds out his hands, and says, "Pelota."

I smile back at Lina, who's eyes are tearing up. "He wants a ball."

"I'll be right back," Liam says. He slips outside.

I talk more with Pablo and find out that he's six and likes soccer. He smiles when I tell him I'm twenty-four and like to cook.

Before I can say more, kids race into the house with gifts in their hands. They show off their new toys to Lina and Andy. Bradley follows behind, smiling and ho-ho-ho-ing.

"Hola."

I glance at Liam standing above us, holding a Ninja Turtle kickball. Pablo jumps to his feet and asks in Spanish if it's for him.

Liam holds out the ball as if reading his reaction. I nod to reassure Pablo. He takes the ball and hugs it to his chest. Lina comes over to us with tears falling. She sniffles. "That was perfect."

Liam laughs. "Thank my G-Maw. She loaded us up with a bunch of extra stuff today. There's clothes out there too."

Lina leaps at Liam and hugs him so hard that his elf ears fall to the floor. Pablo puts them on, making me laugh.

I glance around the room filled with so much joy and holiday happiness. Andy is on the floor playing Legos with some younger kids, a couple of teenagers check out a tablet, and Bradley sits in the recliner with two younger kids on his knees.

When Lina lets go of Liam, he walks toward the fireplace. I follow him and notice a sprig of mistletoe on the mantel. My stomach flips when he looks at me. I nod toward the mistletoe. He laughs nervously and cups his hand around my face. I step closer and tilt my head toward him.

He shifts awkwardly and whispers, "Not in front of the kids."

My shoulders sink, taking my heart down with them. I nod slowly and turn to face the kids. Liam wraps his arm around my waist. I want to lean into him like I did on the ride here, but I'm more confused now than ever.

Was that his way of saying our private kiss actually meant something or his way of saying it was a mistake?

# CHAPTER ELEVEN

*Carmelita*

I try not to enjoy Liam snuggled up to me on the ride back. There's so much weirdness between us right now that I can't get optimistic about our relationship. Speaking of weirdness, it doesn't help that we're riding in a tractor-pulling sled driven by the county sheriff, who is dressed like a cowboy Santa.

"Are y'all coming to the parade tonight?" Bradley asks.

"I'll leave that up to Carmelita. She's been jerked around town a lot today," Liam answers.

I relax against his chest, happy he'd take that into consideration.

"She's got to see the parade," Bradley suggests. He turns to me. "A parade is where all these decorated cars, and trucks, and tractors, and animals ride through town."

I squint, trying my best not to sound insulted. "We have parades where I grew up."

"For real?"

"Yeah, the Parade of Pearls is the most popular."

"That's a cool name," Liam says.

"Thanks. Everyone wears their best pearls and we decorate all the floats with pearls."

"Makes ours sound even more redneck." He laughs.

Bradley scoffs. "As grand marshal, I take offense."

Liam rolls his eyes. Bradley straightens his fake beard and stares at the road ahead. After an awkward moment of silence, he speaks up. "If y'all decide to come, let me know. I'll find you a spot in the VIP section in front of the Pig."

"I appreciate it," Liam says. He pinches my side.

I snap my head toward him, and he winks. My neck and face warm as I smile before leaning my head back against him. I'm thinking I don't want to go to the parade. We need some time to talk about whatever is going on between us.

Bradley whistles along with a song on the radio as we drive the last stretch of road to the city hall. He parks us as close to Liam's truck as possible without getting in the way of other vehicles.

"All right, y'all. Santa's got more work to do. I'm gonna unload what's left of G-Maw's donations inside. I wanted Lina's kids to get first pick."

We follow him out of the cab, and Liam shakes his hand. Bradley pulls him in for a tight hug. "You're all grown up on me, boy."

"Good to see you too, Bradley."

He finally releases Liam, who nods awkwardly. Bradley tips his hat and heads toward the building while we get in Liam's truck. Once we're in the truck, Liam watches Bradley out the window. "Hard to believe I once wanted my sister to marry that guy."

"He's nice," I comment.

Liam laughs, and I join him.

"Let's get back to my house before something else crazy happens."

He puts the truck in gear and turns out of the parking lot. I stare out my window. I've never had to start a conversation with someone about a kiss. Partly because the only person I've kissed before today was Antonio.

Even stranger is that anytime I broke things off with him, he left with a smirk of confidence, as if I'd said we would pick things up later. In his mind—and my parents'—we would. Perhaps I once thought we would too.

Not now.

Even if things didn't work out with Liam and we split in a year's time like the contract states, I don't want to fall back on Antonio. I want to try adult life in America and find a guy I pick, not one a bunch of old people on the island decide is best.

Liam breaks the silence after a few minutes. "So, the Parade of Pearls. Sounds interesting."

I turn from the window. "Yeah. We celebrate Christmas a lot where I'm from, and that's like the grandest parade."

"There's more?"

"Not organized parades, but we have people singing and performing at festivals throughout the holidays."

"Anyone dress up like cowboy Santa?"

I laugh. "Nope."

"Sadly, Bradley's not the only one around here who does."

"Nothing wrong with that." I smile.

Liam sighs. "I appreciate you being so cool about all this. People around here are a little much, and I get that."

"Everyone's been super sweet."

"Sweet, yes. But a bit annoying at times."

"No really, aside from your dad's pregnant comment, everyone's been great."

Liam chuckles loudly. We laugh together down his family's road. Woody adds to our entertainment by standing in his yard waving.

"What is he wearing?"

Liam shrugs. "Looks like those feet pajamas little kids wear."

"Isn't it a little early for that?"

"You never know with Woody."

We continue down the road to his parents' house. His mom is coming out the front door when we park. She waves as we get out. "Hey, kids. Y'all going to the parade?"

Liam glances at me and lifts his eyebrows. I press my lips together. He turns back to his mom. "We're going to stay here for tonight. It's been a long day, and I want Carmelita to see *Die Hard*."

"What's that?"

"Just the greatest Christmas movie ever."

Mrs. Sanderson steps off the porch and rolls her eyes. "It is not a Christmas movie."

"Mama, every Christmas movie doesn't have to have a love interest."

"Name another one."

"*Elf*."

"He gets a girlfriend."

Liam stares at the sky before looking back at his mom. "Okay, *Home Alone*."

She purses her lips. "I'm going early to help Aunt Carla with the cookies at Mary's."

A loud horn beeps behind us. We all turn to a red-and-white van barreling down the drive. It's heavily decorated with Alabama and Roll Tide logos.

Mrs. Sanderson blinks, looking confused. "I didn't expect Nannie and Pop until after Christmas."

The van comes to a screeching stop, slinging gravel. An

older couple climbs out of the front. The woman throws her arms around Liam, then hugs Mrs. Sanderson. "So good to see y'all!"

"You too, Nannie. We thought you were in Branson," Mrs. Sanderson says.

She waves a hand. "Some new couple booked the time share an extra day without notifying everyone, so we had to kill some time before the turnover."

Mrs. Sanderson nods. "I see. I'm headed to town for the parade, if y'all would like to join me."

"I need to see my son first, so he can't say I blew by without him," Pop says.

He's dressed in a Bama jacket and cap—both of which have seen better days. He scans me head to toe, then turns to Liam. "Boy, how'd you get a pretty woman like this?" Then he turns to Mrs. Sanderson. "She does belong to Liam, right?"

Liam's mother nods. "She does. This is Carmelita. They met at school."

He snarls. "Well, if she ain't the only good-looking thing I've seen come out of Auburn."

My cheeks heat up, as I'm not sure how to respond to that. It's evident by his clothing and vehicle that he doesn't hold Auburn in high regard.

He grins. "I'm Joseph, but prefer Pop."

"Hi, Pop, nice to meet you."

"And I'm Remmie." His wife hugs me. "Or Nannie." She giggles.

"Nice to meet you too."

Mrs. Sanderson raises her brows at Nannie and Pop, then turns toward the house. "Come on, and I'll get Joey."

She leads the older couple to the house and opens the door. I expect her to walk in, but she yells from the porch, "Joey, your parents are here."

"Be out in a minute," an equally loud answer comes from somewhere inside.

Bully howls, and the hog grunts. Liam smirks at me. I swallow, trying to read his expression.

"You want to go in the basement and watch a movie or something?"

"Sure."

My body tenses as I follow him around the side of the house past the hog in a pen. It snorts and whines at us. He opens a door at the back of the house that leads to a studio apartment. There's a couch, bed, TV, mini fridge, and microwave. It's not all that different from my dorm room.

I settle on the couch and watch Liam rummage through a cabinet near the TV.

"Ah ha!" He holds up a VHS tape with the words "Die Hard" labeled by a marker. "I still can't believe you haven't watched this."

I laugh. "It doesn't sound like something I'd be interested in."

"Don't judge it just yet." He pops the tape in the VCR and grabs a remote. Then he plops down beside me and drapes his arm over the back of the couch.

It's not around me as much as behind me, but I'm not lost on the fact that we're alone in a basement. Now is as good a time as ever for me to bring up the kiss.

"Liam?"

"Yeah?"

"In your G-Maw's basement, or whatever that was." I'm not sure if it can be called a basement when there's no floor. "Uh, you kissed me."

He turns to me and bites his lip. I study his eyes as I wait for a response.

"I'm sorry if that made you uncomfortable." He scoots an inch or so away.

"It didn't." I turn my body toward him in an effort to assure him I don't want him to leave. "I was curious why you did it. You know, since we weren't in front of anyone to prove that—"

His lips are on mine before I can finish explaining. I melt against him as his hand rests on my back. This kiss is every bit as good as the first—or better, since I'm more convinced he wants it.

Best of all, I want it.

My mind blurs as the stress of our odd relationship hides behind this moment. He wraps his other arm around me and kisses me deeper. I'm lost in Liam until a horrid sound blares beside us.

I jerk and turn to the TV. Liam sits up straighter when it happens again from behind the wall.

"Sounds like someone's in the bathroom."

I press my lips together and try not to gloat at how red his neck is. His lips are also flush and his pupils dilated. He cranes his neck toward a door against the back wall.

We hear a toilet flush, and then the door opens to Lacie wiping her mouth.

"Hey, y'all."

"Are you okay?" I ask.

"Yeah, cow-butt cookies and cinnamon rolls don't mix too well."

Liam snarls, then turns back to the TV. I straighten on the couch and sit next to him. Lacie brings a beanbag beside us.

"So, what are we watching?" She sprawls out on her back and rubs her belly.

Liam frowns at her. *"Die Hard."* He leans over and whispers in my ear, "Which is what I wish she'd do right now."

I laugh.

"What's so funny?" Lacie asks.

"Nothing, we're going to go get some fudge." Liam stands and offers his hand.

I take it and lace my fingers with his. It feels natural now, not for show. We climb the stairs and find his grandparents and dad in the kitchen.

"Liam Joseph Sanderson," Nannie says in a scolding tone.

"Ma'am?" A terrified look crosses his face.

"Why didn't you tell me you got married?"

He palms the back of his neck. "It happened pretty quickly, Nannie."

Pop makes an air gun with his hand and elbows his son.

"Nope, that's the first thing I asked," Mr. Sanderson says.

I swallow. Apparently, anyone who gets married quickly around here has to be pregnant.

Nannie props her hands on her hips. "I would've sewn you kids a wedding-star quilt and got her a ring."

"Liam gave me your ring."

"Let me see, dear." Nannie looks as confused as I am.

I walk toward her and lift my hand. She squints and holds my hand toward the light.

"Oh, I remember this. I gave it to Liam one year for Christmas."

"Yes, it's beautiful," I say.

She lets go of my hand and fans hers dismissively. "It's decent, but not what I'd pick out for my granddaughter-in-law. We get better ones in all the time."

"Better ones?" Either they own a jewelry store or she's really into rings.

"Yeah, at the pawn shop."

"Pawn shop?"

"We normally give him a gun every year, but were running low the year the Democrats took back over," Pop says. "Nobody wanted to let loose of any. Remmie suggested we give him something of equal value to a gun as an investment." He laughs and slaps Liam on the back. "I'd say he got extra interest when he landed a lady like you."

I twist the ring on my finger. Instead of a supposed family heirloom, it's a piece of jewelry from a pawn shop, given in the absence of good guns. I'm not sure whether to feel relief or resentment.

*Liam*

Carmelita stares at the ring I gave her. When I told her it was my grandmother's, I forgot to mention my grandparents own a pawn shop. Maybe she won't hold that against me.

In my defense, it is real. And it's not like I planned on getting married anytime soon. If that ring were worth a new mobile home, I'd have pawned it already.

Good thing it isn't, or we'd never have gotten married.

We both needed something from each other, and so far I couldn't be happier with the way things are turning out.

She smiles at my grandparents and tucks a piece of hair behind her ear to reveal pearl earrings. I watch her describe her job to Nannie, while Pop eats the rest of Mama's chocolate peanut candy.

"I still don't get why a girl as pretty and smart as you would choose to go to Auburn," he says.

I shake my head. He's so obsessed with UA that he believes anything with AU is blasphemy.

"Pop, they have a good engineering program. I'm about to graduate from there too."

He frowns. "I know, don't remind me."

Nannie narrows her eyes, then reaches across the kitchen table and pats my hand. "Don't worry, dear. We will be at your graduation with bells on!"

"Yeah, my bell that plays the Bama fight song."

Daddy widens his eyes at me before turning to Pop. "Dad, do y'all want to ride with me to the parade?"

"Naw, we've got to get on the road." He takes off his cap and a long, thin strand of hair falls. He swipes it over his bald spot and replaces the cap. "We want to go halfway tonight since we've got reservations at the Dolly Parton Stampede tomorrow."

Carmelita grins at me, and I hold back a laugh. Leave it to my family to educate her on all things Dolly Parton.

"I want to hug Lacie first if she's around," Nannie says.

"Okay, I'll get her while you walk out. She's had a few sick spells." Daddy stands and helps Nannie to her feet before going to the basement.

It's hard for me to watch my grandparents getting older. That's the biggest reason I want to move closer to home after I graduate.

All the more reason Carmelita might not want to stay with me long term. She's about to start a great job at Auburn. Nobody in a marriage of convenience would want to move because of her new husband. That would take away the convenience of it.

Nannie hugs me, then Carmelita, one more time. Pop slaps me on the back and gives my shoulder a slight squeeze. In his and Daddy's world, that's equivalent to a hug and kiss.

Carmelita and I follow them to the door, then wave as they leave the porch. I shake my head at the ridiculous Bama van before shutting the door.

I turn to Carmelita and smile. "Now you've met all my grandparents."

"They're nice," she says.

"Mostly. Pop doesn't like Auburn."

"Then I guess we're in this together." She smiles.

I rest my fingertips on her side and step closer to her. The door opens before I can make a move. Collins walks in with Lacie behind him. He's wearing his dorky Santa hat, and she's in some kind of feathered coat, fanning her hands.

"Why are you fanning?" I ask.

"I'm burning up." She fans even faster with both hands.

"Then take off that chicken coat."

She scoffs. "It's fur, and I'm supposed to dress festive to help Aunt Carla with the cookies."

"Babe, you're having hot flashes and your ankles look like an elephant's."

Lacie gives Collins a look that communicates he can go somewhere that will give him hot flashes. He frowns, and I try not to laugh. It doesn't work.

"I'm serious. In my medical opinion, you need to stay in and put your feet up."

He leads her to the couch and props her legs on an ottoman. Then he takes off her boots and socks. Her feet are thicker than tree trunks.

"Whoa."

She snaps her head at me. "I can't help it."

"Where's your ankle?"

She starts to cry. I should've stopped at "whoa."

"It's okay. It's normal to swell near the end of a pregnancy. As long as your blood pressure is good, you're fine." Collins strokes her head like she's a puppy.

"I think I'll be fine if I wear flip-flops."

"No," he says firmly. "You're staying here with your feet up. You need to rest, for you and the baby." He kisses her forehead, then holds the sleeve of her coat. "And take off this ridiculously hot jacket.

She allows him to pull it off, then plops back against the

couch. "Aunt Carla needs someone to dress festively and pass out her new designs."

Collins glances at me, then Carmelita. I blink, then shake my head. There's got to be plenty of oddly dressed people who like cookies in Apple Cart tonight. Why bring me into this?

"Fine, I'll go help if y'all can make sure she rests," he says.

"Deal," Carmelita says.

I sigh, wishing she hadn't agreed so soon. I planned on negotiating staying under the same roof with Lacie, but not watching her.

Collins stands and stares at Lacie. "Promise you'll stay here with your feet up, unless you have to pee."

She salutes him sarcastically. He shakes his head, then turns to us. "Make sure she isn't up doing things. Her feet need to stay elevated." He picks up her feet and shoves a pillow on top of the ottoman before lowering them again.

"We'll keep an eye on her," Carmelita promises.

I wish she'd have said "I" instead of "we." Most of my younger years were spent doing whatever my older sister said. I don't care to relive that at twenty-two.

"Thanks." Collins beams. He gives Lacie a quick kiss on the lips, then rushes out the front door. Either he's worried Carla might get mad, or even he's tired of my sister's constant bossiness.

I've always heard that money brings out the best and worst in people. I think it's pregnancy.

Lacie fans her face with a throw pillow and smooshes her head deeper into the back of the couch.

"Lacie, would you like some water?" Carmelita asks.

"That would be nice. If you can only do a third cup of ice, then water."

Carmelita nods and walks toward the kitchen.

"And a straw, please," Lacie calls out.

I follow Carmelita and find a straw. Mama keeps them in this little round thing in a bottom cabinet, so the odds of her finding it would be none.

I stick it in the glass. "You know, we don't have to take care of her."

"I feel bad. Her ankles look horrible."

"What ankles?"

Carmelita and I laugh together.

"I can hear you," Lacie calls from the couch.

Carmelita bites her lip to keep from laughing harder. Then she brushes past me, and I follow her to the living room. She hands Lacie the glass.

Lacie takes a long drink of her water and sets it on the end table.

"Are you hungry?" Carmelita asks.

I press my lips together to keep from yelling. Of course she's hungry. She eats more often than the hog out back lately. And we don't need to offer to do more than she asks.

"Now that you mention it, some popcorn would be nice. The kettle kind with some of that cheese-powder stuff Mama uses on it."

I turn and go back in the kitchen. It will take Carmelita a week to find the cheese powder.

I have to dig through several layers of Mama's spice cabinet before finding it myself. Lacie better appreciate all this. One day when I have a pregnant wife, I'm going to call her and ask for favors.

Carmelita's small frame with a large belly pops into my mind. I quickly shake that thought. I don't need to jump ahead to us having kids. First, I need to convince her to stay married to me.

I shake the popcorn bowl to spread some of the cheese to the bottom. Carmelita would be a great mother. She was amazing with that little Spanish kid at the children's home, and she's taking care of Lacie.

Maybe one of these days, when I'm done with school and she's legal in the country. Hopefully by then, I can charm her, or at the least wear her down.

When I return, she's sitting on the couch near Lacie, laughing about something on TV. I reach over the back of the couch and hold the bowl between them.

"Thanks." Lacie grabs it with both hands.

"Careful." Carmelita straightens the pillow under her legs.

Lacie squirms and sets the giant popcorn bowl beside her. Carmelita scoots down to make more room for it, leaving no room for me on the couch.

I sit in Daddy's recliner and stare at the TV. It's one of those Christmas love story movies. Not the kind Mama watches that make people cry, but the kind that tries to be funny but comes across corny.

Somewhere between the guy in the sweater vest falling down a hill and the firefighter confessing his love for his best friend, I fall asleep. With any luck, I can enjoy an evening alone with Carmelita in my dreams, because it ain't happening in real life.

# CHAPTER TWELVE

*Liam*

After taking a long shower, I look for Carmelita. I woke up late this morning to find out she'd gone shopping with my mom and sister. Collins had gone along to make sure Lacie didn't overdo it. That left Daddy and me here to check our guns and clean the tools for the hog killing.

So a typical Christmas break afternoon in my family.

"Carmelita seems like a nice girl."

I stare at Daddy. He's not one to make comments like that—ever. Maybe sharpening pork-chop knives brings out his vulnerable side. If he has one.

"Thanks?"

"I'd prefer you'd told us before getting married, but it looks like you made a good choice. Shows real maturity."

I half smile. That might be a compliment.

We work in mutual silence for the next few minutes.

Daddy sharpens and I clean. We've done this routine so many times that we're a well-oiled machine.

Headlights blind me, and I shade my eyes. The vehicle cuts off, and Collins hops out of the driver's seat. He hurries around and opens the front door for Lacie. Mama and Carmelita climb out of the back with arms full of shopping bags.

"I don't even want to know what they spent." Daddy shakes his head. "One of the biggest headaches in marriage is your wife shopping."

I mentally count Carmelita's bags. It doesn't really matter to me as long as she can cover the trailer payment. We haven't legally combined any finances, and I doubt we will, given our unique situation.

Mama walks in the garage first and kisses Daddy on the cheek. No doubt a peace offering for spending whatever she spent.

"I'm going to put these things away. You boys need to clean up before G-Maw's."

"Yes, ma'am," Daddy and I say in unison.

That's when I realize she has us both trained.

We work on the next knife as Collins walks by holding Lacie like a toddler. Daddy straightens his glasses and stares at them.

"She's got bad ankles right now," I say once they're in the house.

He shakes his head. Carmelita walks up next with two big bags and three small bags. I've learned with jewelry and ammunition that smaller bags don't always equal less expensive.

"What are you guys doing?"

"Preparing for the hog killing," Daddy answers. He holds up a newly sharpened knife and beams with pride as it glistens under the overhead garage light.

"That's a lot of knives," she comments.

"We prepare all the meat that day, right after the kill. These will be used to slice and dice different cuts."

She glances down at her bags. "I hope what I got for G-Maw's is okay. Your sister and mom said I could only spend ten dollars."

"Yep, that's the spending cap."

She shrugs and starts inside. I check my phone.

"You can go ahead and get cleaned up," Daddy says. "These knives aren't about to grow legs and walk away."

"Thanks."

I take a quick shower and head to my bedroom for a nicer shirt than I usually wear. Carmelita is by my bed, checking out the Auburn posters on the wall. She flinches when I enter.

"Sorry, I didn't mean to snoop."

"It's fine. There's no telling what you'll find in here." I chuckle.

She holds up a well-worn ice skate and raises a brow.

"Prank."

She nods, then scans the room. "It's so camouflaged in here, I don't see how you can find anything."

"That's why I'm letting you decorate the new home."

"Good call." She smiles.

I swipe a hand over my damp hair. Now that I'm married to a hot girl, I should consider combing it more often. I'll take care of that after finding better clothing than the plain white T-shirt I'm wearing.

"I didn't mean to fall asleep last night and leave you with Lacie."

"Don't apologize. She only asked for one more snack before Collins came home."

I shake my head.

"Really, she was no trouble. I enjoyed the movie, and I could tell you were bored."

"Not with you, just with the movie."

"Good to know." She smiles wider.

I smile at her, then open my closet. In the back are a few shirts I reserve for church and funeral homes. I pull a blue one that old ladies say match my eyes . . . just in case. Maybe it's wishful thinking, but I swear Carmelita's been staring at my eyes.

I put it on over my undershirt and button it.

"Do we need to dress up?"

I turn around to her watching me. "No, I just thought I'd not look like a redneck slob for once."

She laughs. "Whoever told you that you look like a redneck slob?"

I shrug.

"What are you taking for a gift?" she asks.

"This pocketknife I don't use anymore."

"A used knife?"

"Yeah, new it would be worth way more than ten bucks."

"Liam," Mama's voice calls from the doorway. She pokes her head in my room and sees Carmelita.

"Oh, sorry to interrupt." Her cheeks flush and she smiles.

"We're just talking," I say.

"Could you help me with the tea in a minute?"

"There was still a ton of tea there yesterday."

Mama's face scrunches with worry. "I don't want us to run out. It's just a few jugs."

"Okay."

"Thank you, baby." She disappears down the hallway.

I sigh and look at Carmelita. She giggles, then follows me out of the room.

As I expected, the kitchen counter is covered with jugs of

tea. I grab an armful, and Carmelita takes the remaining two jugs.

"Mama, can you get the door?"

She turns from washing something in the sink. "Certainly."

We follow her to the back door and pass Daddy in the garage. He shakes his head at the hoard of tea. Mama frowns at him, and he stands.

"Give me a minute to wash up." He sets down the knife he's holding and goes inside.

Mama opens the back of her SUV and shuffles bags to make room for the tea. I unload the jugs and shake out my arms. Carmelita hands me hers to squeeze into the space.

"What's all these bags?" she asks.

"Dirty Santa gifts."

"I need to put mine in as well."

"Don't worry. Joey's still getting ready, and I'm sure Collins has Lacie resting," Mama says.

"Is she really that bad?" I ask.

Mama shrugs. "I tend to think everyone makes a bigger fuss over their first baby, but Collins is a medical professional. That could make him extra cautious."

"Or extra crazy," I add under my breath.

Mama cuts her eyes at me, and I stare at the tea. "Is that all?" I ask.

"I believe so."

I shut the back hatch before she can give me any more glares. Carmelita leads the way back inside, where voices come from the living room. Unfamiliar voices.

I crane my neck to see one of those weird survival shows on TV. Daddy loves to see people suffering out in the wild. He sits in his recliner and makes comments about how he could do better.

Collins and Lacie are on the couch, and if she's not asleep, she's close. Carmelita comes back with a small box.

"What's that?" I nod at the box.

"I can't tell you."

"I helped her shop," Collins says proudly.

"I can't wait to see it, then." I widen my eyes. Carmelita laughs.

Mama rushes in with keys in her hand. She stops beside me and looks at everyone. "Y'all ready to go?"

Collins sets Lacie's feet on the floor like she's breakable, then helps her stand. Daddy focuses on the TV, not moving an inch.

"Joey," Mama says louder.

He doesn't move. She frowns at me. Lately, she's been on him about getting his hearing checked. He argues that she's so used to her own dad not hearing anything that she's paranoid any man of a certain age can't hear. Then she accuses him of having what she calls "selective hearing." His usual comeback is if he had that, he'd never hear Misty.

I'm waiting on this conversation to begin when Mama takes the remote from the arm of the chair and turns off the TV. Daddy turns to her.

"It's time to go."

"Oh." He stands and takes the keys from her hand.

I laugh to myself. Daddy isn't going to let a little hearing loss keep him from driving instead of Mama.

If I can manage to stay married as long as them and only argue about hearing loss and who's the better driver, I'll consider that a win.

Collins announces that he will drive Lacie separate in case he decides she needs to rest. I open the back door of Mama's SUV for Carmelita and put my hand on her lower back as she climbs inside.

We sit together in silence as Daddy drives less than a mile

to G-Maw's. As far as I can tell, Carmelita likes all my family. Tonight will be the real test, when all the random extended relatives and family friends come to G-Maw's and fight over cheap Dollar General gifts.

If anything could make her leave me—and the country—that would be it.

*Carmelita*

Woody's yard is extra lit tonight, if that's even possible. The flashing lights make it look like downtown Vegas. Well, I've never been there myself, but according to TV shows, it's that bright.

The Santa calls after us when we open the car doors. Mr. Sanderson opens the back and starts gathering teas. Liam helps him, and I help with the gifts.

"At least we have enough light so we don't trip over a goat." Mr. Sanderson frowns at Woody's yard.

I get the sense he finds it tacky, especially compared to all the matching, more traditional decor in their home.

"Woody's got a lot of Christmas spirit," Mrs. Sanderson says as we weave around vehicles and chickens to the front porch.

"He's got a lot of something," Mr. Sanderson counters.

Liam laughs.

"I don't remember chickens when we came here before," I say.

"They randomly get loose, mostly at night. Same as the goats," Liam answers.

Right on cue, a goat bleats loudly, and I almost drop the boxes in my arms. It's perched on a porch step, staring at us.

Mrs. Sanderson marches ahead and shifts the boxes in her arms to one side. She grabs the goat by the neck and shoves it off the porch. The goat bleats at her, then disappears behind the house.

When we're all on the porch, it only takes one knock before someone swings open the door. Woody stares up at us in what's either an elf costume or very fitted pajamas with a hood. Maybe both. His two tiny dogs are wearing suits to match his.

Where does he find stuff to fit a grown man and a five-pound dog?

He steps back and nods as we enter and squeeze against the wall. Everyone stares at us like we're the new kid at school. G-Maw comes from the kitchen and hugs us all.

"Robin, you didn't have to bring more tea. We have plenty in the cellar." G-Maw hugs her and takes her gifts.

"Oh, it's no problem."

Mr. Sanderson slides toward the kitchen with his tea. Liam does the same, and I follow him.

"Ain't you gonna introduce your new girl?" someone calls from the living room.

Liam sets the tea on the counter and takes the gifts from me. "We may as well get this over with so we can have a somewhat peaceable night."

"Okay." I follow him back to the living room.

He sets the gifts under a small fiber-optic tree. *So that's what was pricking my legs when we smooshed inside earlier.*

Now all eyes are on me. Some of these people I know, some I've met briefly, and some are total strangers. One couch is full of kids of all ages, scanning me up and down. It's a little intimidating.

Liam puts his hand on my lower back, and it soothes my

nerves. I try and focus on him rather than all the eyes in the room.

"You've met my branch, along with Woody, Misty, Earl Ed, G-Maw, and G-Paw."

"And me." Jeffrey pops around the corner holding a cookie.

Several people frown at him.

"Misty is holding Piper, and the two boys by the door are Conner and Ricky, also her kids."

Two boys dressed head to toe in baseball gear sit by a back door with a Nintendo in front of them. One has enough gold chains around his neck to fill a jewelry store display case.

"That's Michael, her oldest, and his wife, Krystal, and their daughter Colleen."

"That's Krystal with a K like the restaurant." The blond woman smiles widely.

I return the smile, curious why I need to know how she spells her name.

"Ashton's still getting ready, and Tommy is still on house arrest." Misty grins.

Liam raises his brows. "Those are Misty's other two kids." He turns. "You know Aunt Carla from the cow-poop cookies."

Carla smiles and waves an oven-mitted hand.

"Her husband and Earl Ed's dad, Earl, is somewhere."

"Hey, nice to have you," a voice calls from the kitchen.

We turn to an older man cleaning a gun at the kitchen table. G-Maw comes by with a tray of rolls.

"Son, I told you to use the dining room table. This is where we fix our food."

"Sorry, Mama." He starts gathering his materials to move.

"That's their daughter, Carly."

A teenage girl looks up from her phone and waves.

"The lady sewing is G-Paw's sister, Aunt Bea."

An older lady sleeps in a corner rocker with some knitting needles in her lap. She's dressed like the cast from *Little House on the Prairie*, minus the bonnet.

"Everyone else is a Stevenson, including all the kids." He nods toward the couch full of stares. "They live on the road connected to ours."

The man and woman nod in unison without saying a word. I guess I won't know their first names.

Liam takes a deep breath and exhales with a smile. "Everyone, meet Carmelita, my wife."

Some smile, others whisper, Krystal gasps. All while I swoon. Something about the phrase—"my wife"—coming from Liam's mouth unleashes a swarm of butterflies throughout my body.

After a short pause, the comments and questions explode.

"Where did y'all meet?"

"Do you like baseball?"

"What's your favorite part of the pig?"

I blink, then Liam holds up a hand to shush everyone. "She can get to know all of you soon enough. Let's give her some space."

Some pout, and others whisper. Earl steps in the room and whistles loud enough that a dog howls in the distance. Everyone quiets down, and G-Maw shuffles in front of him.

"We're going to say the blessing and eat," she announces.

Earl stands and everyone bows their heads. I do the same and listen as he thanks God for family, food, and guns. He spends way more time on guns than anything. At last, he says, "Amen."

I lift my head to people piling up by the kitchen. I hang back with Liam.

"Sorry about the interrogation."

I shake my head. "It's fine. That's just a lot of people to meet at once."

The door swings open to Bradley in his uniform, minus the Santa stuff. I peer through the window to make sure nothing is going on outside.

"Is everything okay?" I ask.

"I certainly hope so. It's my dinner break." He winks at me. "Liam."

Liam shakes his hand. "Bradley."

Bradley tips his hat and falls in the back of the food line, which stretches to the living room couch. Woody steps beside us with the dogs.

"Hey, can you two watch Taco and Belle while I run home and get my gifts?"

Neither of us answer, but he shoves a dog at each of us. I get the one with the green hoodie, and Liam's is wearing red and white stripes. Woody bolts out, and the screen door slams behind him. I flinch, and my dog growls. I pet it gently until its teeth disappear behind thin gums.

"I wonder if this is what it's like to have twins?" Liam says.

I laugh. The line shortens so the only other person in the living room is Aunt Bea. I back onto a chair near the wall, and Liam joins me, sitting on the arm. Both dogs seem content for the moment.

The door opens again to an older couple carrying Styrofoam boxes and a wrapped gift. The man jerks his head around the room, then grins when he sees us. "Liam, how are ya, boy?"

"Good, Paul."

He turns to the woman with him and nods toward us. She follows him to where we're sitting.

"Dot and I wanted to get y'all a little something for the marriage."

"How sweet." I smile, and the lady beams.

"You didn't have to do that," Liam answers.

"We insist," Dot says.

She holds out the gift in her arms. Liam and I stare at the dogs before setting them both on the floor. He takes the gift and gives me a cautious glance. I untie the ribbon and slowly lift the lid on the box.

It's a set of mason jars with candlesticks. I lift the mason jar first and discover the assumed candlestick is stuck to the bottom of it.

"Oh thanks." I return it to the box.

"It's mason jar wineglasses. So you can toast." Dot sounds so proud of this find.

Liam clears his throat and covers the box. "Thank you both."

"Don't mention it," Paul says. "I need to thank y'all. After I saw how cute those were, I decided to order more for my store."

A group of kids comes in with plates and sits on the couches and at a nearby folding table. Paul jerks his head toward the kitchen, then at Dot. "Come on, darlin', they've started eating."

She lifts a hand. "Congratulations, nice to meet you."

"Thanks, you as well."

The door creeps open and Woody's striped leg pokes through. He slides it open, then collapses toward a cooler he's holding. Liam stands and braces the cooler so Woody doesn't fall. They lower it to the ground, then Liam rejoins me on the chair.

Woody's dogs rush toward him. He pets each one, then stands and yells, "Everyone, I have a little something for y'all!"

Those who aren't already sitting in the living room gather around.

"Since everyone enjoyed the butts I smoked last year, I got a ham for every family."

People smile and watch with anticipation as Woody opens the cooler. He pulls out an armful of canned hams and hands them to Krystal. She stares at them.

"Go ahead, take one and pass them. One for every family."

She fakes a smile and hands her husband a ham. Her toddler takes it and bites on the edge of the can, as if teething.

"I'm guessing the smoked butts that made such an impression last Christmas weren't canned," I whisper in Liam's ear.

"Nope." He stands and offers me his hand. I take it, and he pulls me to my feet. "Perfect timing to eat some real meat G-Maw made."

The only person left in the kitchen is Paul, loading the plates he brought with food. He scrapes the last bit of mashed potatoes before I can reach the spoon.

"Oh, my bad, little lady. Here you go." He slops a spoonful off his plate, raking some okra along with it and dumps it on mine.

I swallow and force a pleasant face. Liam raises his eyebrows. "Let's go claim a corner in the den before Woody tries to shove a ham at us."

"Good plan."

I follow him to another tiny living room off the kitchen. A slightly larger fiber-optic tree with an angel on top sits in the corner. Presents are stacked high beside it. Liam settles in front of some boxes, and I sit beside him.

He holds up his red Solo cup. "To enjoying a romantic

dinner of turkey, non-canned ham, and vegetables in the mood lighting of a Dollar General tree."

I clink my cup against his and laugh.

"Actually, that one came from my store."

We turn to Paul in the doorway. He nods toward the tree, then moves on with a stack of to-go boxes. We burst out laughing. This is the most entertainment I've had in a long time.

# CHAPTER THIRTEEN

*Liam*

Our romantic dinner was short lived.

I took about two bites before Aunt Misty's sons dove on a beanbag across the room and started wrestling. Then Uncle Earl escorted Aunt Bea to a nearby comfy chair to save her spot for Dirty Santa.

At least none of them cared to carry on a conversation with us. Aunt Bea picked up her needles and started humming a hymnal. I forget the name of it, but I'd bet a Coca-Cola or a cell phone it has the word "blood" in the title.

G-Maw comes through with Mama, and they shuffle gifts. Mama picks up one and squints at the card.

"This is to Jeffrey?" She wrinkles her forehead. "Who brought him a gift?"

"Oh, I wrapped that," G-Maw says.

"Why?"

"He keeps coming around."

"So do Bradley, and Paul, and the Stevensons," Mama argues.

"And I have things for them as well." G-Maw smiles.

Mama shrugs. "Okay, these are going to the living room."

She returns with different gifts. Jeffrey's sons have rolled toward the tree, and G-Maw swats at them. "If you're going to wrestle, go in the yard."

"But the goats will get us," Ricky says.

"Serves you right," she says sternly.

They stand and sigh, then trudge toward the kitchen. Aunt Bea holds up a long scarf-looking thing and hums louder.

Mama moves a package and winces. "G-Maw, look at this. I think it's leaking."

G-Maw examines the wrapping, which is moist in the corner. "Hmm, must be one of those slime-making kits."

Mama shakes her head, then carefully puts it beside the other gifts. She wipes her hands down her pants. "I think we're ready to make numbers," she announces.

G-Maw counts the gifts once more. "Good, I'll get Lacie to write them." Then she marches into the kitchen with Mama behind her.

I scoot closer to Carmelita. "Do you play any gift games back home?"

"We have Monito Monita."

"Huh?"

She laughs. "It's Secret Santa. We draw names and buy whomever you get a secret treat."

"Some people do that over here too."

"What do they call it?"

"Drawing names."

She laughs harder.

"I have to warn you, the gifts for this are pretty crappy."

"Like used knives?"

I narrow my eyes. "That's one of the better gifts. I'm talking like stolen road signs and two-dollar bills."

"I've never seen a two-dollar bill." She sits up straighter, as if curious. "How much is it worth?"

"Uh, two dollars."

She smirks. "Guess I had that one coming."

People start piling into the tiny den. I have no complaints about moving so close to Carmelita that she's practically in my lap. Earl Ed plops down beside me and sighs.

I can tell he misses Mackenzie, so I don't ask if she's still working. I'm sure everyone over forty will ask about her tonight anyway.

The homeschool kids sit as close to the pile of gifts as Mama will allow. They get way too excited over this game.

Uncle Earl gives his famous whistle, and the chatter slowly dies down. The only person still talking is Aunt Misty.

"I told you, only my salon salary counts, not the side money from Dolly Parton impersonations. If you want to pay less child support, you need to take me to court."

Earl clears his throat, and Misty looks away from Jeffrey. Her face reddens when she realizes everyone is waiting on her to hush.

"Sorry about that. Continue, Earl," Jeffrey says.

Misty rolls her eyes and marches toward Woody. Uncle Earl takes his time explaining every rule of the game as he does every year. I'm certain Carmelita is the only one in the room who hasn't played, and also the smartest in the room. Still, he goes into detail about the stealing rules and getting number one.

Lacie steps forward with a Solo cup and starts shaking it. He gets the hint and wraps up his speech.

"Raise your hand if you're playing, and keep it raised until I get to you." She shuffles around, holding out the cup for everyone with a raised hand.

When she gets to Mr. Stevenson, he drops his hand to her belly. Lacie freezes and her eyes bug.

"Sorry. I have a bad habit of feeling babies kick."

His wife pulls his hand away from Lacie and selects two numbers for them. Lacie rushes past them, almost tripping over Krystal's crossed leg as she swings it back and forth.

Ms. Dot gets the coveted number one. Fair enough, since it's her first time playing with our group. She starts us off by opening a wrapped bottle of laundry detergent. Mrs. Stevenson perks up at that. I guess if I had seven kids, laundry detergent would be high on my wish list too.

We continue going around the room, one number at a time. I get my own knife, and Carmelita shakes her head.

"It's totally legal to open your own gift," I tell her.

She's a few numbers after me and gets a round block of cheese.

"Oh." She fakes a smile and sits it beside her.

Collins beams. "I picked that up from the dairy when we visited Lacie's alma mater, Mississippi State. It's the same kind we served at our wedding." He wraps his arm around my sister, and they smile at each other.

"Thanks." Carmelita nods.

I bite my tongue to keep from laughing. With the ten-dollar spending cap, a lot of food gets circulated in this game.

Aunt Bea opens a framed photo of Nick Saban. Several people tell her to check the back of the frame for money or a gift card. After she fumbles around with the frame a few minutes, Daddy speaks up.

"It's just the photo. I brought that."

Mama frowns at him. "Your Daddy gave you that yesterday."

"Yeah, from the pawn shop."

Mama crosses her arms.

"What? It's got his signature," Daddy argues.

Aunt Bea stares at it in confusion. A few turns later, Jeffrey relieves her of it. Michael steals from him, and Jeffrey opens a hot plate. Krystal smiles proudly.

"You'll love that. We use it to cook all kinds of things at the shop."

I whisper to Carmelita. "Michael runs a welding shop."

She nods.

Jeffrey examines the box. "Thanks, Krystal, but I'm gonna use it to warm bats."

She turns to Michael. "I thought bats carried Covid."

"Baseball bats," Michael corrects.

She smiles, then stares at the ceiling in confusion.

We're far enough in the game that people are stealing more than opening. The only present left unopened is the leaky one Mama shoved in the corner.

The last number belongs to one of the homeschool kids. His eyes are fixed on the gift.

"Look around, and see if there's anything you like," his mom warns.

He does a quick scan of the room, then dives toward the gift. Carmelita pulls her legs to her chest so he won't hit her. Scraps of wrapping paper fly our way when he rips it open. He pulls a tinfoil ball out of the large box.

Everyone is silent as he peels back the tinfoil.

A nostalgic aroma fills the air when he opens it to one of Woody's smoked butts. Everyone oohs and ahhs.

"I could still afford to smoke one," he says.

People start negotiating with the kid, making side deals

about swapping after the game. He hugs the meat close, fear in his eyes.

Bradley steps to the center of the room, a piece of pound cake in one hand. "Hey, hey, settle down."

Everyone stops talking except for Jeffrey, who's beside Misty with the hot plate.

"I'll give you ten more dollars a week, if you help me buy Conner that commemorative Trump 2024 compression sleeve."

Again, they notice every eye on them.

"Sorry," Jeffrey says. He waves the hand not holding the hot plate. "Carry on."

"I think we're forgetting that Dot still gets a choice before we end this game." Bradley swallows his last bite of cake, then swipes his hands together. "Everything in the room is still fair game."

Carly points to Bradley's seat, which holds a half-eaten cake. "Then why did you go ahead and eat some of your gift?"

He smiles, then continues. "Ms. Dot, what in here would you want?"

Dot asks to see the skillet G-Maw is holding. She examines it closely and seems interested. Paul looks worried and whispers something in her ear. She hands the skillet back to G-Maw.

"I'll take the Boston butt."

The little boy stands and sighs in relief before handing over the unwrapped meat. She hands him the laundry detergent, and his mom cheers.

"This is a better ending than most," I admit to Carmelita.

She lifts the block of cheese. "Speak for yourself."

"You mean you're not going to make us something delicious with that?"

She shrugs. "We'll see."

People compare their gifts and pick up wrapping remains as the night winds down. I don't think anyone noticed Misty left until her return in full-on Dolly Parton gear.

"Woody, are you ready, dear?" She props a hand on the doorway to the den.

"Yes, we are." His tone is high as he bounces the dogs in his arms. I guess that's supposed to be their voice.

"Misty, where are you going like that at this hour?" G-Maw asks.

"Caroling, Mama, like we do every year."

G-Maw walks to the edge of the room and pats Carly's shoulder to move her away from a door. She pulls out a large Carhartt coat like G-Paw wears to feed the animals.

She tosses it at Misty. "Wear this so you won't get cold."

"Mama, it's like sixty-eight degrees outside."

"Well, you look cold." G-Maw scowls at her, then moves to the kitchen.

I turn to Carmelita. "That's old Southern women talk for not having enough clothes on."

"Duly noted." She smiles and rests her head against my shoulder.

I wrap my arm around her waist and sit contently as my crazy family carries on eating random gifts. Carmelita hasn't complained or been weirded out—at least that I know.

Even more reason for me to make sure this relationship works out.

*Carmelita*

Literal banjos play in the background as I help G-Maw put away the food.

I've always heard the expression about banjos playing in the South meaning something negative. I'm not sure what that means, but what's playing in the living room isn't half bad.

The entire homeschool family plays stringed instruments and brought them along. Most of the teenagers and other non-family have left.

Krystal comes in the kitchen with an armful of plastic plates. She drops them in an industrial-sized trash bag hung on a cabinet handle.

"Thank you, Krystal," G-Maw says. Then she turns to me. "I have such good help with all y'all spry young girls." She pats me on the shoulder, then slides by and grabs a gallon of tea with each hand.

"Hey, Robin?"

Mrs. Sanderson pops her head in the kitchen. She's holding another large trash bag, this one filled with wrapping paper.

"Do you want to take this tea home?"

Mrs. Sanderson shakes her head. "No, just keep it."

G-Maw frowns.

"We'll take it." Paul comes by with an armful of Styrofoam plates. "Grab those, will you, Dot, darlin'?"

Ms. Dot reaches for the tea, but G-Maw sets it on top of Paul's plates. It bends the top one before Dot can get it off. G-Maw turns to Krystal and me and smirks.

"Y'all have a good night," she calls as they open the front door.

Liam comes in and takes the bag from his mom. I watch him talk with her, then our eyes meet. He smiles. Something splashes my face, and I jump back.

"Sorry." Krystal winces. "I thought I could ring the sink."

She nods to a half-empty cup dripping on the counter. Then she grabs a towel to mop up the mess.

Liam hurries to the kitchen and finds a napkin. He blots my face where the drink splashed against my cheek. I stare at his eyes until an annoying squeal echoes behind us. Everyone stops cleaning up, and the string instruments stop strumming.

Misty rushes toward the front door with Woody and their dogs. They leave, then the screen door reopens. The Carhartt coat flies through and lands in the house, then the door slams shut again.

I pull back the ruffled curtain to see what caused such a commotion. Woody and Misty climb into the back of a white van pulled in the drive.

"What's Wisteria Worship Center?"

"The church," Liam, Mrs. Sanderson, and G-Maw answer in unison.

I scrunch my forehead and watch the van maneuver around Woody's lawn ornaments before heading down the main road.

"They're going caroling with the church," Mrs. Sanderson says. "Which is probably why G-Maw didn't want Misty getting cold."

G-Maw shakes her head and buries her face in the refrigerator. It's so full, the light is barely visible. If Paul hadn't taken so many plates home, we'd never get all the leftovers inside.

"I'm going to take this wrapping stuff to the burn pile," Liam says.

"Okay, son, we're almost done in here." Mrs. Sanderson wipes down the countertops.

I help Krystal bring the rest of the food plates to the trash. The music slowly starts up again with a familiar Christmas song.

Earl Ed and Michael come into the kitchen with a deck of cards. Collins follows with Lacie beside him.

"Mama, can I ride back with y'all? They asked Collins to play cards."

"Sure, honey. Where's your dad?"

Lacie points to the den. Aunt Bea, Mr. Sanderson, and Earl are all in easy chairs, asleep.

Carla shakes her head. "I can tell Earl is sitting up. Otherwise, we'd have heard snoring by now."

Liam walks in, smelling like a bonfire. "Anything else to burn?"

"Nothing but time," Earl Ed says.

"Come play poker," Michael says.

Liam looks at me as if asking permission. I don't mind if he plays, and I don't think he should even consider if I mind, so I say nothing.

He pulls out a chair and sits across from Collins.

"Okay, I'm going to grab my purse, and anyone wanting a ride to the house now can go with me." Mrs. Sanderson leaves the room.

"What about Daddy?" Lacie asks.

"Let him sleep. He can catch the next bus," she calls from somewhere in the back of the house.

We can barely hear her over a fiddle solo to "Oh Holy Night."

Lacie loops her arm through mine. "You can ride home with us. Trust me, their card games are boring."

All four guys glare at her. She shrugs and leads me to the door. Mrs. Sanderson follows, saying goodbye to everyone. The Stevenson family nods, now playing for an audience of only G-Paw. He seems to enjoy it though.

A fire flickers in the distance, and the flames flare when we step off the porch. "Should someone be watching that fire?"

"I've got it." Bradley steps out of the shadows and lifts the brim of his hat.

"Okay." I lean back, startled.

He follows us to Mrs. Sanderson's SUV. "Have a great Christmas Eve Eve, ladies."

"You too." Mrs. Sanderson side hugs him and gets in the driver's seat.

The ride lasts just long enough for Lacie to describe her unborn child's nursery. Apparently, Collins is big on safety features and baby proofing everything. That doesn't surprise me.

She collapses on the couch as soon as we're inside. Mrs. Sanderson goes to the kitchen with her dishes, and I stop behind Lacie.

"Lacie, do you need anything?"

"No, thanks." She smiles and props a pillow under her feet.

Or tries to. She struggles to reach the pillow, as her belly only allows her to bend so far. I circle the couch and straighten the pillow under her feet.

"Thanks, Carmelita." She rests her head against the back of the couch. "I don't know why you like my brother, but I'm glad you do."

I laugh. "He's got a lot of good qualities."

She shrugs. "The older he gets, the better he acts."

I nod and go down the hall to my bedroom, or our bedroom, which was once Lacie's bedroom. Either way, the room where I'm staying.

The TV comes on, and I hear Mrs. Sanderson. I peek out the door and notice her going into the living room. Curiosity gets the best of me, and I slide down the hall into Liam's old bedroom.

There's nothing of value, unless you count guns. But I

somehow feel closer to him in here. It's very camouflage and very Liam.

I spend the next few minutes looking at photos of him with dead deer and snooping in his closet, which is nothing but more camo. Satisfied that he isn't hiding anything extremely weird or creepy, I go to Lacie's old room for some clothes. I'll get my shower out of the way while everyone else is occupied.

Tomorrow is Christmas Eve and sure to be busy.

The Christmas songs playing at G-Maw's run through my mind as I wait on the water to warm. I step under the showerhead and pull the curtain after humming a verse of "It Came Upon a Midnight Clear."

I'm shaving my last leg when I hear something. I stop humming and stick my head out of the curtain. Liam is standing in front of the toilet, dropping his jeans.

I scream and jerk the curtain around me, falling back into the tub. Water sprays me, cementing the vinyl curtain to my body like nori to sushi.

"Are you okay?" Liam turns off the faucet and reaches for my hand.

I tuck my hands close to my side and squint to not see his unzipped jeans. He wastes no time reaching down and hoisting me into his arms. I open my eyes wider and meet his gaze.

"Are you hurt?"

I shake my head.

"Good. I'm sorry." He gently sets me on the toilet, zips his pants, and heads for the door.

"Where are you going?"

He stops at the door and looks back. "Outside to pee."

I blink and watch him leave, locking the door behind him.

It takes me a minute to process what just happened and

to realize I need to peel off this shower curtain and rehang it so I can finish my shower. I have one and a half shaved legs and still need to wash my hair.

Luckily, the curtain didn't break, as the rings snapped off with it. I unroll the hot plastic from my body and rehang it, then finish my shower as quickly as possible.

At least I found a way to clear the Christmas songs from my head. Worrying if Liam saw anything besides the curtain —and what—circles my brain while I run the hair dryer.

Once my hair is dry enough to serve as fireplace kindling, I ease into the bedroom. Liam isn't there. I go down the hall to check if he's in the living room. I'm almost there when he calls behind me.

"Carmelita."

He's standing in his old room's doorway, wearing nothing but shorts. Thankfully, shorts that don't have a zipper. I swallow and step toward him.

"I'm sorry about what happened. That was stupid of me. My parents drilled into my head at an early age not to pee outside when we have company. I had to go pretty bad after all G-Maw's tea."

I nod. "It's okay."

He crosses him arms over his bare chest. I force my eyes not to look at it.

"I'm going to sleep in here tonight so you won't be weirded out. I know neither of us is used to living with someone, and I don't want to make you more uncomfortable."

I press my lips together, not sure how to respond. Am I embarrassed and nervous about what happened? Yeah. But mainly because I like Liam. Like, like-like him.

After a long pause, I manage to squeak out, "Good night."

Then I retreat to Lacie's old room and climb into bed. I

stare at the plastic stars overhead, trying to sleep. Instead, I toss and turn as I'm reminded of tossing and turning in the tub like a fish out of water.

That's a pretty accurate description of how I feel after swimming in uncharted territory with Liam.

## CHAPTER FOURTEEN

*Carmelita*

I wake up to the smell of coffee grounds and the sound of plates clinking. If Mackenzie were here, we could film a Folger's commercial. If they still make those.

This would be the time of year they'd air, along with that Hershey's commercial playing bells.

Soon as I make my bed and brush my teeth, I peek in Liam's room. The door is open and the bed is somewhat made. I crane my head to see if he's standing near the closet.

Nobody's there.

I assume he's in the kitchen, but it's Mrs. Sanderson and Lacie.

"Good morning, Carmelita." Mrs. Sanderson grins at me before pouring coffee. "Did you sleep well?"

"Yes, ma'am," I lie.

When I finally did fall asleep, I had nightmares about worst case scenarios. One where I fell in the shower without the curtain, one where I caught Liam mid pee, and worst of all, one where both those happened, but he turned and peed on me.

So I guess it could've been worse. Not that it makes me any less embarrassed or confused.

He'd said we're not used to living with someone. Very true, considering I'm an only child who was happy to ditch a roommate. Liam had a whole mobile home to himself before marrying me.

Even after I moved in, we had separate bedrooms and bathrooms. This week has forced us to spend more physical time together, and forced me to evaluate my feelings for him.

"Want some coffee?" Lacie asks.

"Sure."

Lacie brings a mug and sits across from me. She slides it slowly, then watches intently as I drink it.

"It's good," I say after swallowing.

She laughs. "I don't mean to stare. Collins won't let me drink coffee right now because of the baby and all my swelling, so I try and enjoy it through others."

I lift my chin. That's strange, but after getting to know both of them, I totally get that. I sip my coffee and try to ignore Lacie drooling over it a few feet away. Looking out the window above her head helps.

"Do either of you know where Liam is?" I ask.

Mrs. Sanderson joins us and sets a plate full of muffins on the table. Lacie grabs for one, and she swats her hand. I lean back in shock.

"What are you, a heathen? Say the blessing."

Lacie bows her head and mumbles a quick prayer before snatching a muffin. She drops it in front of her. "That's hot."

"Serves you right," Mrs. Sanderson says. Then she picks up one using a napkin. "Muffin?"

"Thanks." I take it in the napkin. "So, Liam?"

"Oh yes, dear. He's at the Christmas tree shoot."

"The what?"

Lacie rolls her eyes. "The men go out to Jack's place and play this shooting game. They hit dots of paint on a dirt bank painted like a Christmas tree. It's really a waste of time, but they do it every Christmas Eve."

Liam didn't mention this event to me. I guess he didn't want me there. It does sound boring, but I'm a tad hurt that he didn't ask. Or at the least, tell me where he was going this morning.

Last night must've bothered him too. Maybe I don't look so hot wrapped in a wet shower curtain.

I take a bite of my muffin and think of something to say that won't show my hurt. "Um, if it's a game, what does the winner get?"

Lacie tentatively bites into her muffin and smiles when it isn't too hot. "Nothing," she says with a mouthful.

"I thought Michael won a gun last year?" Mrs. Sanderson says.

Lacie shakes her head. "That was something between him and Earl Ed, but it never manifested into anything."

"Well, us ladies are going to get ready for tonight." Mrs. Sanderson sips her coffee and turns to me. "Carmelita, you're welcome to help us make appetizers for the progressive dinner."

"Thanks."

"I'll be glad to share all my recipes with you." She smiles before biting into a muffin.

"That's very sweet of you."

"Of course, honey, you're family." She smiles wider.

My insides warm at her acceptance. I just hope her son still wants me to be family. "What time does everything start?" I ask to get Liam out of my head.

"Everyone will arrive here at six for appetizers, then we

go to G-Maw's for the main course, then Carla and Earl's for dessert."

Liam pops back in my head, so I try a milder deterrent. "Do either of you go shoot guns?"

"We both have before, but it's been a while."

"It's not that fun," Lacie says, staring at my empty coffee mug.

I focus on the tractor-covered Christmas tree behind her to not feel guilty about my caffeine fix.

"We'll have plenty of fun making fudge here," Mrs. Sanderson says.

"Isn't that a dessert?"

She laughs. "Honey, in the South, a lot of foods overlap."

I wrinkle my forehead. "So sweets for appetizers?"

"Yes, and we eat breakfast and brunch food anytime."

"With potatoes in many forms," Lacie adds. "Also, macaroni and cheese is considered a vegetable."

I lift my chin. "Then that's why it's listed under veggies at a lot of Auburn restaurants."

They both laugh.

"Don't worry, Carmelita. We'll teach you everything you need to know to survive as a Southern belle."

Lacie smiles and nods in agreement with her mom. I smile and finish my muffin.

It's bad enough that I'm falling for Liam without knowing if he's serious about me. Even worse, I'm falling in love with his family too.

I pray the standoffishness will die down soon and my mishap didn't cause us any permanent damage.

*Liam*

# QUEEN OF MY DOUBLE-WIDE TRAILER

. . .

I aim my rifle and fire a bullet into the center dot. Dust flies from the dirt pile and everyone cheers. Bradley shakes his head, then steps up to the line. He nods, acknowledging my shot.

Nobody else wanted to go against him, so I did. Collins got stuck with him the first year he came, but that was more about Bradley trying to play alpha male and win back my sister. Funny why he thought that was a good idea, since she wasn't even here to watch. Last year Uncle Earl challenged him, but this time he and Daddy decided to go against one another as usual.

Bradley fires a perfect shot to one of the smaller dots painted near the center of the tree. Applause rings out. He bows.

I don't expect to beat a guy who spends most of his spare time at target practice. However, I didn't want to go against any of my family. This trip has made me appreciate family more than ever.

Especially my wife.

That word rings in the back of my head as I fire another bullet. This one doesn't hit as squarely as the others. It's safe to say I'm distracted.

I'm staring at a dirt pile disguised as a tree with ornament targets, but the image overtaking my mind is Carmelita spread across the bathtub floor with the wet shower curtain suctioned to her slim curves.

I should've thought twice before reaching for her waist and pulling her into my arms. Only when I realized my pants were unzipped did I realize how creepy that might come across.

Weird, since we are married.

But then we aren't. Not in the way married people

should be.

I'd intended on slowing toward that with kisses and hand holding and all that. Who knew it would be so hard to date your wife?

One more round of shots with me flubbing it, and Bradley easily takes the victory. The loss doesn't bother me, but the reason for it does.

I may have made her really, really uncomfortable. Like to a level where she will not want to be in a room alone with me ever again.

How would that work back in Auburn?

Will we have to create a schedule of when to use the kitchen and living room? That could get awkward ASAP. And would she let me eat anything she cooks?

In only a few weeks, I'm spoiled by Carmelita's food.

I sit on the tailgate of a truck while Collins shoots against Krystal. She's the only girl here, and he shoots like one. I've never seen her shoot, but she grew up in Mississippi and spent her adult years before meeting Michael in a casino.

With that background, she's sure to have more gun experience than my Atlanta born and raised brother-in-law.

Jonah takes a seat next to me. He's shooting against Michael next. "You got married, huh?"

"As did you." I raise an eyebrow.

He smiles. "Yeah, man, but I was engaged a while. Yours kinda snuck up on everyone."

I lift a hand. "She's not pregnant."

Jonah bursts out laughing. "I didn't think she was."

"Some people have asked."

"I'm sure." He leans back on his elbows and laughs again.

Krystal hits the hardest target and everyone cheers. She jumps up and down, holding the gun. Jack rushes over and takes it from her. He pats her shoulder. "I think it's best to end this round. Krystal's far enough ahead, she wins."

## QUEEN OF MY DOUBLE-WIDE TRAILER

She jumps again, this time without a gun. Collins crosses his arms. "No fair, I still had another shot."

"Okay, take it," Jack says, moving Krystal out of the way.

Collins inhales and squares his shoulders before shooting one more time. He misses his target by several inches and lowers his head. Krystal jumps one more time, then high-fives Michael.

"What did I win?" she screams.

"Bragging rights," Jack tells her.

Her face falls a little.

Jack steps toward the dirt and yells, "Who's next?"

"What made you decide to get married?" Jonah asks once the commotion dies down.

I look him dead in the eye. "I needed a place to live."

He laughs so hard, he rolls over in the truck bed. I laugh with him. When I say it out loud, it does sound like I'm kidding.

At least that comment ends his questioning.

We watch Daddy beat Uncle Earl by a slim margin. Jonah stands and stretches. "It's my turn to beat Michael."

"Good luck."

Daddy joins me on the tailgate.

"First time you've beat Uncle Earl in a few years. Congratulations."

"Yeah, I can't wait until the next Alabama Gun Club meeting."

"You think they'll dethrone him?"

Daddy chuckles. "No, but maybe worship him slightly less."

I shake my head. Uncle Earl is like a local celebrity when it comes to old men with guns. He even has his own gun room at home. And by room, I mean large enough to live in, not some closet with a combination lock.

"You about ready to go?" Daddy asks.

"Sure." I try and sound casual.

In reality, I'm nervous about facing Carmelita. She was asleep when we left. I swing my legs and stare at the ground in front of me.

Collins comes over and hands his gun to Daddy. "Thanks, Mr. Joey."

Daddy frowns at the gun, then puts it in the truck. I start loading the other guns in the truck, and Collins climbs in the back.

"We'll need to practice next year before you shoot that gun again," Daddy says.

"Yes, sir," Collins agrees.

He's smiling, but I see through Daddy's offer. It isn't so much out of wanting to spend more time shooting with Collins as it is Daddy's embarrassment of a girl beating his son-in-law at a shooting competition. A girl who once thought two-dollar bills are worth ten dollars.

My boot crunches something on the floorboard when I step inside. I move my foot and pick up a small branch with white berries. "What's this?"

"Some of Earl Ed's mistletoe," Collins says. "He shot it out of a tree earlier. He gave me some thinking Lacie might like it. You can have it though. She doesn't seem to appreciate anything right now that isn't edible."

Daddy smiles genuinely. "Don't worry, Collins, that will end when the baby comes."

"I hope so."

"You boys have a lot to learn about women—marriage, babies, and all that. The most important thing you can know is you'll never know it all."

I stare at the branch and twist it between my fingers. Daddy makes a good point. I'm clueless at best about my relationship, including if it's a real relationship.

Maybe I should hang on to this mistletoe and see if it brings me some luck.

*Carmelita*

Today was like a crash course in being a Southern belle.

Mrs. Sanderson and Lacie told me tons of Southern phrases and their meanings while we made three flavors of fudge and prepped the house to accommodate a crowd of mingling guests.

Everything made sense until we set up five different power strips in the kitchen. Mrs. Sanderson explained that a lot of appetizers come in Crockpots. She also explained that making fudge for an appetizer is easier on her, since she can hold some back for the dessert rotation.

We stay so busy that I barely have time to think about Liam and what happened.

That is until the door opens and I hear boots across the hardwood floor. He and his dad trudge in with an armload of guns, followed by Collins holding ammo boxes. All are dressed in head-to-toe camo. I've seen Liam like this before, but it's an odd look on Collins.

"How'd it go, boys?" Mrs. Sanderson asks.

"I barely beat Earl, Bradley barely beat Liam, and Krystal clobbered Collins," Mr. Sanderson answers.

"Krystal?" Lacie asks.

"Hey, that girl's intimidating." Collins's voice is stern as he tries to defend his loss.

Lacie dips her head and hides a laugh.

Collins sets his shells on the counter. "Don't laugh. I'd like to see you shoot against her."

She clears her throat and puts on a serious face. "I was needed here."

He rolls his eyes, then turns to Mrs. Sanderson. "Has she been taking it easy?"

"Yes. She's been sitting on a stool at the stove stirring fudge most of the day."

He nods and smiles.

Liam and I lock eyes for a few seconds. I try and read his thoughts, but can't. We don't know one another well enough for that. I wish we did. Maybe with time. Unless, of course, he spends the next year avoiding me.

Ugh. That sounds like a lot of fun.

"Could I get you boys to do some stuff outside for us before you get clean?" Mrs. Sanderson asks.

All the guys mumble some sort of agreement. She wastes no time giving her husband tasks concerning the hog and dog. She asks Liam and Collins to move some tables from the basement.

I smile at Liam as he passes me, and he smiles back. Collins stops in front of me. "Take care of Lacie. Make her rest."

"Okay."

I spend the next half hour sitting with Lacie in the living room, making sure her feet are elevated. Collins glances our way every time they pass with another folding table.

By the time they're done, I'm needed to help spread tablecloths across them. Liam disappears to get ready, leaving me clueless about how he feels.

We work until it's time to get ourselves ready. I freshen my makeup in the bedroom, hoping he will come in, but he doesn't. He stays in the living room with Collins.

When I join him on the couch, he half smiles. Is that an

apology smile or an "I feel sorry for you" smile? I'm so terrible at reading him.

I return his smile and try to relax. There's not much I can ask in front of Collins. I keep hoping he will get up and check on Lacie, but he doesn't. Instead, he makes loud, nerdy comments about how they made the movie on TV.

He finally walks away.

I consider questions to ask Liam about last night. As I'm deciding between "How are you doing?" and "Did you sleep well last night?" the doorbell rings.

Liam sighs and goes to the door. A group of people enter with covered dishes and Crockpots.

I guess this conversation will have to wait.

## CHAPTER FIFTEEN

*Liam*

Carmelita meets my gaze from the living room. I press my lips together in an apologetic response.

We haven't been together all day, and before we could be alone, the herd comes in. At least she didn't move away from me when Collins left the living room. That's a good sign, right?

She stands and walks toward me as Mama enters the room.

"Welcome, everyone. Make yourselves at home." Mama grabs the remote and puts it on one of those channels that's more like a radio station. It plays Christmas music without words and shows a fireplace on the screen instead of actual videos.

Carmelita meets me at the door. I start to put my hand on her back, but resist. I almost flashed her, then sucked her to me with nothing between us but a thin curtain. She needs to make the first move.

"Liam, I heard you got married."

"Yes, ma'am," I turn and answer Mrs. Oakley.

She taught me in high school and wasn't my biggest fan. The way she looks at Carmelita tells me she's shocked I married someone so . . .

Let's just say I dated a lot of bleached-blond girls who didn't always wear enough clothes.

Temporarily forgetting my vow to let Carmelita make the next first move, I wrap my arm around her waist. "This is Carmelita. We met in engineering classes."

"Impressive." She smiles at Carmelita. "I'm Eva Oakley. I taught Liam in high school."

Carmelita smiles. "Nice to meet you."

I cup my hand around her waist, proud of my beautiful wife who is wearing a normal amount of makeup, with weather- and event-appropriate clothing.

She doesn't flinch, which is a good thing. It may all be for show, but I'll take it as her not being totally terrified of me.

Mrs. Oakley talks a few more minutes. As she's walking away, a couple comes to introduce themselves to Carmelita. It goes this way the entire time at our house.

We manage to migrate toward the kitchen for appetizers, but get caught up in another conversation with Jack and Jonah.

I shift my focus from talking about last night to getting though tonight. I sigh with relief when it's time to head to G-Maw's for round two.

Collins comes behind us and wraps his arms around our shoulders. "You two can ride with us."

Just great. I can't even get Carmelita alone for a two-minute car ride. I help some of the older people load their pots and plates in their vehicles, ignoring Paul stacking plates. He can steal leftovers without any help.

Carmelita is waiting in the back of Lacie's van when he and I finish helping everyone pack up. I should've protested that they all brought food in without our help, but Mama wouldn't stand for that.

I climb in beside Carmelita and fight the urge to put my hand on her knee. Since coming here for Christmas, I've gone from not touching her at all to kissing her every chance I got, and now I'm scared to touch her again.

I wish she'd just blurt out whether she wants me or not. It's much easier when the girl comes on to you.

Collins slams on the brakes, sending my face into the back of my sister's seat. I'm reminded of him wrecking on our road the Christmas I met him and regret not wearing a seat belt. Dude doesn't pay attention.

The headlights blind Woody, who's directly in front of the van, wearing a reflective vest and Christmas light necklace. He holds a hand to his eyes and uses the other to point us toward the edge of G-Maw's yard.

All the vehicles are lined up rather than randomly parked up and down the road as usual. I guess he's doing a good job.

Collins parks, and the doors slide open. I wait for Carmelita to get out and fist my hand to keep from putting it on her back.

Woody fans his hands toward the house, almost hitting Collins in the face.

"We know where to go, buddy." He frowns and hurries past Woody.

We fall in line and wind around the other vehicles to the Astroturf porch. This time I do touch Carmelita slightly. She's between Lacie and me, and my sister wobbles like a peg-leg pirate.

Again, she doesn't flinch, so I count that as a small win.

# QUEEN OF MY DOUBLE-WIDE TRAILER

People come from the kitchen with plates and find places to sit. We join the line still forming to fix plates. It stalls near the entrance to the kitchen. Jonah is a few people in front of us with his wife, Carolina. He grins at me, then looks above my head and nods.

I follow his eyes to a twig of the same berries I brought back from the shooting game. Mistletoe.

Someone hung a decent-sized branch of them from the old ceiling tiles with fishing line. Thanks to G-Maw's short ceilings, if the string had been any longer, it would've hung on my cap.

Jonah wiggles his eyebrows. I narrow my eyes, warning him to move on. The line is backing up and more people are paying attention to us . . . including Carmelita.

I suck in a breath and glance down at her. She stares at me, then turns to Jonah. Her eyes follow his to the mistletoe. I swallow hard as she lowers her head enough to meet my eyes

I silently pray she can read my willingness to kiss her.

When she leans the slightest bit my way, I dip my head toward hers. Our lips brush gently.

Jonah starts chanting "kiss" like a little pervert. More people join him. I stay locked on her lips without moving a muscle. Maybe it's peer pressure from all the chanting and need to prove our marriage, but she kisses me.

Like for real kisses me.

Right in the middle of G-Maw's house, under a mistletoe hung by fishing string.

She kisses me in a way that says she's not just doing this for show. She wants this kiss as much as me.

I relax and enjoy the moment, not caring who's watching. But it's short lived when a piece of Saran Wrap suctions to my forehead and pulls me back.

I blink my eyes open to Bradley pulling me away from Carmelita and the hallway.

"What in the?"

"Big dog, cool it down. We're trying to get these people through the line so we can eat and play the Saran Wrap game."

He pulls the plastic away from my face and winks. Then he heads for the den with the wrap blowing behind him. He doesn't say anything until G-Paw gives him a dirty look. "Don't worry, I bought this roll from DG earlier today."

"You're such a wasteful generation," G-Paw scolds.

Bradley chuckles and continues toward the living room. I make my way back to Carmelita, or at least try. The line has progressed and nobody wants to give me back my spot.

It's not like G-Maw didn't make enough pots of chicken and dumplings to feed the entire county. I take my place in the back and find Carmelita talking to Jonah and Carolina after I make it through the line with my food.

Carolina gives me a stern look. "How come you told her about us, but not us about her?"

I shrug. "We didn't date long."

Carmelita lifts one corner of her mouth in a half smile. I concentrate on her lips and replay our kiss in my mind. That kiss answered all my questions and erased all my worries.

G-Maw's bell rings, calling everyone's attention to the living room. I stop daydreaming long enough to hold my bowl of dumplings steady for her to pass me. She stands in the center of her rug and scans the room.

"I know some are coming in late and still eating, but we need to get started on the Saran Wrap game. If you want to play, Bradley has it ready in the den."

"What's that?" Carmelita asks.

"The game I told you about where we unwrap Saran

Wrap to get gift cards, dollar bills, and random stuff from the dollar aisle at every store."

She nods.

"We can sit and eat while everyone else is playing if you want."

She smiles. "Sounds good to me."

I lead her to the corner of the living room, where a TV tray is set up between two folding chairs. Nobody else is nearby except for G-Paw, who sits in protest of the game.

He thinks Saran Wrap is expensive and not to be toyed with. I sit next to Carmelita and study my grandpa before speaking. His hearing aids are turned down, or we'd hear them squeal from here.

"I'm sorry about last night."

She shakes her head. "No, it's fine. I get why you wouldn't want to share a room with me."

"Wait, what?" That is *not* what I was thinking. "I meant I'm sorry for snatching you up like that and making you uncomfortable. I thought you were hurt." I wince. "And for the whole peeing thing."

Her cheeks redden. "I thought you didn't like what you saw, so you've been avoiding me."

I laugh. "Didn't like what I saw?"

"Yeah, the whole wet shower curtain thing."

I laugh again. "Quite the opposite. I was afraid you thought I was a creep for first coming in there with my pants undone, then grabbing you."

She lowers her head, then slowly looks at me.

"I didn't want to stay in the same room with you and have you think I was going to try something."

"Thanks, I appreciate that."

"You're welcome."

She rakes her fork around her plate, then looks at me

again. "So it wasn't anything about you not liking me?" Her voice is hesitant.

I try not to laugh, even though I find it ridiculous she'd think such a thing. "Did you not get the message I just sent by a kiss?"

She blushes even more, making me smile. "Good to know we feel the same way."

I take a long drink of my tea and smile. "You have no idea."

It's nice to finally know my wife likes me too.

*Carmelita*

I can barely eat, and it's not because the dumplings G-Maw made are nothing like the kind we eat. They're mushy, but quite tasty.

Despite the delicious home-cooked meal, my mind is more on Liam than food. A mixture of relief and excitement swirls inside of me after finding out he's attracted to me. Even better, he wanted to be a gentleman and give me space. That means more to me than anything.

Space is something Antonio never understood.

Numerous times, he'd try and hold my hand or kiss my cheek when I said, "Let's just be friends." It's like he thought he'd wear me down eventually. The arrogance of that alone makes my skin crawl.

One thing Antonio never had was humility.

Liam takes a bite of his biscuit and smiles at me. I smile back and imagine life when we get home. Our real home, not his parents' house. The way things are going, we could have a real marriage, starting with a real relationship.

Laughter comes from the other room, and G-Paw turns the TV louder.

"They must be having fun in there," I say.

"I don't know what it is about people around here, but they get really competitive when cheap merchandise is involved."

"Speaking of, do people register for wedding gifts at Paul's store?"

Liam almost spits his tea. "Not to my knowledge. But it's not like I attend any wedding showers. Except for one Jonah had with guys and girls. He registered at Buc-ee's."

"The gas station?"

"Yeah, they have like house stuff inside. It was Carolina's idea."

"Huh." I shake my head. "There's still so much I have to learn about Alabama."

"That's one subject I can actually help you with." Liam grins.

We finish eating as a crowd comes through the house. Most everyone has something in their hand. A gift card, small toy, or pair of socks.

"Odds are if either of my parents got a gift card to the outdoors store in town, it will show up in someone's stocking tomorrow morning."

I smile. "That's good."

"You'd think. But five dollars won't buy anything but a few fishing worms or a pack of gum."

A couple of young kids run by, playing tug-of-war with a long string of Saran Wrap. G-Paw closes the legs of his recliner rather loudly and stomps into a back room, slamming the door.

"And that's our cue to go to Aunt Carla's. If we wait any

longer, we'll have to help clean up and hear G-Paw talk about the Great Depression."

I stand and take our plates. Lacie meets me at the trash bag in the kitchen. She cranes her neck toward the living room. "Where's G-Paw?"

"He went in a room and closed the door," I tell her.

"Good, we can sneak out."

That man must really hate Saran Wrap.

Lacie dumps her plates in the bag and takes my arm. For a very pregnant woman with bad balance, she maneuvers us through the crowd like a champ. She stops at the door, where Collins has Liam. We exit together and spot Woody with his dogs on the front porch.

He says bye to us in a fake voice that I'm assuming he meant to be the dogs'. We all give him polite yet awkward looks and head for the van.

Liam reaches for my hand when we settle in our seats. I smile to myself, content to have him close to me again. We pass his house and continue down a part of the road I haven't traveled.

Music and lights appear after several yards. It takes me a minute to realize the lights move to the beats in the song. Everything Liam and Lacie told me about Carla's house comes to mind. It's every bit as big and grand as they described.

Christmas-colored lights shine on a large fountain in the center of a cobblestone entrance with landscaping that would rival Disney World's. This is the place you'd expect someone parking cars, even a valet. But it isn't necessary with plenty of space to park on either side of the house.

Collins drives toward the edge of the yard and parks near a row of boats. We climb out and walk to the front of the house. When we're within a few feet of the walkway, lights twinkle beside us. Not only are they synchronized to the music, but also to our movements.

The front porch could be a magazine cover. Heavy greenery outlines the double doors like the entrance to a jungle. They're at least a few feet taller than the ceiling at G-Maw's. My eyes gravitate upward when we go inside, to a ceiling at least double the height of hers.

A loud boom comes from the side, and I jump.

"They must be watching something in the theater room," Lacie says.

"Theater room?" I shouldn't be surprised after the light show outside.

My phone rings. Collins shakes his head as I reach for it. "They should really turn that down."

"No, that's me." I lift my phone. My eyes widen when I read "Mama" across the screen. "Excuse me."

I walk to the opposite end of the foyer toward a decorated tree and some chairs before answering. It's easier to get privacy here, unlike at G-Maw's. I swipe to answer the call and sit in a wingback chair. "Hello?"

My heart pings when Mama's voice comes across the line. I haven't talked to her in about a week. She was upset about me not coming home for Christmas.

But before I can get all sentimental about missing her, she takes her upset up a notch—or ten. "Who is this boy you're with?"

*Well, hey, I love and miss you too.* "Excuse me?"

"Don't play naïve, Carmelita. I saw photos of you on the internet with an American boy. Photos of you two hugging." She gasps. "In front of a row of metal buildings."

"That would probably be modular homes."

"I don't care what it is, why are you hugging some boy your father and I don't know?"

My skin itches and I squirm in the cushiony chair. Not knowing what to say, I stall. "Where did you see the photo?"

"On the internet."

"No, Mama. Specifically."

"Some weird social media page about those box homes. Someone sent it to me and asked if it was you."

I pinch the bridge of my nose and sigh.

She continues. "The whole island's seen it now, and I've been getting all kinds of questions."

I swallow and blurt out the words before I lose my nerve. "He's my husband."

Deadly silence makes me fear she's had a heart attack. "Mama?"

"You lied to me."

"I didn't mean to." My skin burns like it's eating itself from the inside out. I've never lied to Mama before, and now I've lied about lying.

"Come home."

"Let me explain."

"Come home." A long breath of anger. "You have twenty-four hours or we're sending a plane."

I choke. "Yes, ma'am."

The phone clicks, and I sit frozen, trying to process what just happened. With the phone still to my ear, I blink, sending a stream of tears down my face. My cheeks burn as they roll down my face and neck.

I turn to the sound of footsteps on the marble floor. Liam stares at me, concern all over his face. I lower the phone and tuck my lips in when they start to tremble.

He rushes over and kneels beside me.

My lips quiver. I stare into his pearl-blue eyes and find enough strength to say, "She knows."

He tilts his head. "Who knows what?"

"Mama. She knows I'm married."

His eyebrows raise.

"And she's given me a day to get home before she sends a plane for me."

"Don't it take you a day to get there?"

I exhale through my nostrils. "That's why she specifically said twenty-four hours."

Liam straightens his cap, then stands. "I guess we need to go, then." He offers his hand and pulls me to my feet. "We can stop by the house and pack our things."

I rest my hands on his chest. "Not *our* things, Liam. I can't let you go. They're mad at me. I can't let them take this out on you. I've got to grow up and do this alone."

His features scrunch with confusion.

"Trust me. It's better this way. You don't know how they are."

He nods slowly and wipes a tear from my face with his thumb. I close my eyes and commit his touch to memory. Once I'm on Oval Island, I can't guarantee I'll ever be back.

# CHAPTER SIXTEEN

*Liam*

The last thing I expected to do tonight was drive Carmelita to the airport. More like ride along with Earl Ed as he takes her to the airport, since he was headed there to pick up Mackenzie, who's flying in tonight for the rest of the holidays.

We share the back seat of his truck in silence, our hands interlocked. I can feel the fear and tension in her fingers. I'd do anything possible to make it disappear.

The entire time she packed her things, I offered to go with her or call her parents or go alone in her place. She insisted that would only make things worse and this is something she has to face head-on, alone.

I halfway wonder if it's a cultural thing. Us Americans would prefer to outsource everything we could—including our pain.

However, Carmelita wouldn't dare pass the buck on to

someone else, even me. I bite my tongue and refrain from asking once more as we turn toward Birmingham.

While we gathered her things, Earl Ed managed to find a flight leaving in a few hours. I choose to believe it's a Christmas miracle to help her out and not a sign that we're destined to be apart.

He gives me a sympathetic face when we stop at a traffic light. I half smile and pat Carmelita's knee with my other hand. She sighs and lays her head on my shoulder.

The exit sign for the airport comes into view after we turn onto the interstate. I hold her hand a little tighter, like doing so will keep her here. If only that would work, I'd have Bradley handcuff us together and throw away the key.

Earl Ed creeps across the airport parking lot. My stomach knots with every row we pass. He parks close to the front and gets her bags.

"Let me help."

He shakes his head. "Just take care of her." He gives me that same sad face like someone ran over his dog.

I pull Carmelita under my arm and walk her toward the entrance behind him. Christmas decorations greet us and people inside hug and say their greetings and goodbyes.

My arm muscles flex as I cradle her closer. I'm not ready to say goodbye.

Once we're close to the security checkpoint, Earl Ed turns around. "Mackenzie is down that way. I'll let y'all talk or whatever while I go get her. I'll swing by here, Liam, to get you."

"Thanks."

He lets go of Carmelita's luggage and walks in the opposite direction. We find a spot nearby and sit in silence. I stare at a Christmas tree and think of the one Carmelita bought for the trailer.

Knowing we'd be here for Christmas, I wasn't going to

bother with one. But she'd come home with a smaller one and a bag full of decorations. I enjoyed looking at it every night, since it symbolized her. Every decoration, including the tree itself, was her style and her decision.

Seeing it without her there will be downright painful.

She sighs, and I give her knee a gentle squeeze.

"I didn't want them to find out like this."

"Not that it matters now, but when did you plan on telling them?"

She shrugs. "After the holidays, and after we—"

"What?"

"Figured out if this was going to be a one-year thing or a forever thing."

I watch her beautiful face fall, and my heart aches. Not just for us, but for her. My parents didn't like me getting married quickly, without telling anyone. I can only imagine how they'd feel if I were a girl living in a foreign country.

"Carmelita?"

"Yeah?"

"I'm here as long as you'll let me be."

A few tears bubble in the corner of her eye. I swipe them away with my thumb, then gently kiss her forehead. I pull her into my chest as she sniffles softly.

It's time for her to go through security if she wants to make it to her flight. I hug her tighter before letting her go. When we pull apart, tears trickle down her face. I lean in and kiss her. The tears wet my face as we kiss like we may never get to again. I try not to think of that being the case.

I peel away from her like a snake shedding its skin. Without her, a part of me is missing. She wipes at her eyes one last time, then hurries to the security area with her bags behind her.

We lock eyes one last time as she goes through. I stare until I hear my name. I turn to Earl Ed holding Mackenzie's luggage with one hand and her hand with the other. I swallow the jealousy bubbling inside me and walk toward them.

"You all right, buddy?" he asks.

I shake my head. Mackenzie drops Earl Ed's hand and gives me a quick hug. I try my best to smile, then follow them to the parking lot.

Nobody says a word as we walk under the street lights and get in the truck. I throw my head back against the seat and close my eyes. Mackenzie says something about her mom, then about her last job. Earl Ed says things about the progressive dinner and how they don't have to go to the candlelight service if she's tired.

My head pounds as I recall every detail Carmelita's told me about Oval Island. Her family is well-off and well-known. They're best friends with the family who runs the place . . . Antonio's family.

I swallow back vomit when his name pops into my head. Carmelita will be half a world away with a rich, handsome guy who she has a lifetime of history with, while I'm stuck in Wisteria, Alabama, singing Christmas carols and killing a hog.

Maybe I shouldn't go to the candlelight service. It's hard to be in a worshipful mood when your wife leaves and there's not a thing in the world you can do about it.

*Carmelita*

Jet lag doesn't begin to describe the way I feel landing in the Philippines. I've had two connecting flights spanning eighteen hours including layovers, or more if you factor in the time change, and I still haven't made it to my island. That will require another smaller plane.

I pull my bags to a bench and settle in where I routinely meet Marino. He's the pilot who transports pearls for my family's business. He's also our go-to pilot for anything personal.

Running home before my mom causes a scene concerning my secret marriage would qualify as personal.

I twist Nannie's ring around my finger and choke back a few tears. Even if I wanted to cry, I doubt my face could handle it. My eyes are red and swollen from crying steadily since I left Birmingham.

A woman with a tiny dog walks by, then a family, followed by an older couple. If I had any tears left, the older couple would make them fall. They hold hands and walk slowly as if they're the only ones in the world.

What I'd give to be with someone that long.

"Carmelita?"

My entire body numbs like I've overdosed on happy gas from the dentist. However, instead of relaxed, I'm tensed by that familiar voice. It doesn't sound like Marino. It sounds like . . .

"Antonio?"

He flashes his perfect teeth and walks toward me, arms open wide. I stay planted on my bench, hands in my lap. He ignores my body language and hugs me anyway.

His arms drape around my shoulders like a wet blanket. I cringe internally as I wait for him to step back.

"I can tell you're exhausted."

I am, but I'm also a lot of other words I don't care to say.

## QUEEN OF MY DOUBLE-WIDE TRAILER

Most of which aren't safe for church and are directed toward him.

"Let's get you to the island." He holds out a hand.

I keep my hands plastered to my side and stand on my own. Not wavering, he grabs both my bags.

"Where's Marino?"

Antonio blinks, as if surprised I'd question why he's picking me up. "With his family, of course. It's Christmas."

"Then why aren't you with your family?"

"We both know there aren't that many pilots on the island. Besides, you are my family." His eyes cut to the ring on my hand.

I make a fist to keep from losing my cool. I'm not his family, and I never will be. He needs to realize that and move on.

Due to exhaustion and frustration, I follow him blindly to where he parked his family's jet. We climb inside, and I let him chatter as he loads my bags. Some young people whisper nearby, and one takes a photo of the plane with her phone.

Just great. I go to rural Alabama and stick out for cultural differences from those around me, then come home and stick out for being around a popular person in my culture.

Antonio has slowly become the face of Oval Island, and everyone on every island knows that, including the mainland.

I buckle up as he gets the plane in gear. At least this flight isn't long. If my brain weren't half asleep and half occupied with Liam, I'd have caught a ferry. Instead, I'm alone in a jet with my rich ex-boyfriend like a reality TV date.

My nostrils flare when Antonio smiles at me. I put on the fakest semi-smile to appease him, then watch the water from the window. Our island is lit up like a Christmas tree. I perk up when the decorated palm trees get large enough to distinguish the colors in their lights. Before we started landing, it resembled a colored blur, although beautiful.

"You've missed quite a few festivities."

"I know, but we still have many left."

"I'm just glad you found a flight to get you here before tomorrow."

I wrinkle my brow. Tonight is Christmas.

"The Parade of Pearls," Antonio clarifies.

I lift my chin. "Of course." For the first time since leaving Liam, I genuinely smile. Then I quickly turn to the window so Antonio won't think I'm directing it toward him.

We land in the field by his house, which I'm sure was intentional. I get using their runway rather than the one in town since my house is next door, but I'm fully aware I'm also on his property.

Once he shuts off the engine, I gather my things with record speed.

"Here, let me help you." Antonio takes a bag from me, slowly dragging his hand along mine in the process.

*Cool it, Casanova. I've seen enough Hallmark movies to recognize your subtle game.*

He flashes his pearly teeth, and I drop my eyes to my feet. My well-worn On Clouds, complete with dirt spots and holes in the toe, are a stark comparison to his shined dress shoes.

Even as a teenager, Antonio dressed the best he could for any occasion. We couldn't play tennis in the backyard without him wearing matching wristbands and shorts, along with his monogrammed towel and water bottle. The guy is like a walking advertisement.

And he has been an advertisement for many local businesses, including the jewelry stores that sell our pearls.

I ease away from his fancy feet and exit the runway

carrying only my purse. If he wants to carry my luggage, he can.

My focus is white Christmas lights outlining the roof of my house. I make a beeline toward our property.

"Carmelita, where are you going?"

"Home for Christmas. I thought that was evident." I don't bother trying to tame my sarcasm. What's the use? The quicker I get the point across that I don't want him, the better.

The worst part about Antonio's family home housing generations of governors is that the security is top notch. That's usually a great thing, but not when you're trying to escape.

I make it to the front of his house and the edge of the yard to find the perimeter gate closed. It's every bit as tall as the front doors of Carla's home, except made of metal.

"Carmelita, wait," Antonio calls out behind me.

He's a few yards away with my bags.

"Unlock this gate so I can go to my yard."

Our property touches theirs on the other side of the gate. I've never felt so close, yet so far from my destination.

"Hold on a minute."

"No, it's late and I want to shower and see my family. I've been on three planes and walked a country mile from the last one."

"Country mile?"

I roll my eyes. "Something I picked up in Alabama."

He snarls. I'm certain Alabama is a curse word to Antonio, and possibly my mother at this point.

He continues toward me. There's nowhere to go but up —literally. I step on a curled rod of the iron fence and then another, climbing it until I'm at the top.

"Carmelita, be careful! If you'd wait on me."

"Nope." I swing my leg over, dropping half the contents of my purse when my upper body follows it.

I descend as quickly as I can to a few feet above the ground, then jump. The gate swings open as I'm bent over gathering my belongings. I grab what I can and hurry across the lawn to my driveway.

My mom is in the living room reading when I walk through. She frowns at me, then looks concerned. "Thank you for coming home."

I nod. "I'm sorry I didn't tell you."

She frowns again. "We need to talk."

I fumble with the strap of my purse and prepare for an earful. The sound of a suitcase rolling comes from behind me. Antonio has let himself in and brought my bags.

I narrow my eyes as he greets my mom with a hug and kiss on the cheek.

"You left these." He smirks at me.

"Thanks." I snatch the handles, not giving him time to graze my hand.

He says something else to my mom, and I take that opportunity to rush upstairs with my bags. It's hard enough to explain to my parents why I didn't want to come home—even harder when the reason is standing in our living room.

## CHAPTER SEVENTEEN

*Liam*

"Son, are you okay?" Daddy hasn't stared at me this hard since the time I got a concussion in football.

"Yeah." I sigh. "Actually, no."

"I didn't think so. When you got your shirt caught in the sausage grinder, I knew something was messing with your mind."

"Sorry about that." I shake my head. Stupid mistake, especially for someone who grew up helping kill hogs.

He tosses another log on the fire and sits in the lawn chair beside me. We both stare at the flames for a few seconds.

"Is everything okay with Carmelita's family? I know y'all had to rush her home."

My stomach sours at the word "home." I like to think of her home as our trailer, but deep down I know it's not. It's on that stupid gem island with Antonio. I poke the fire with a stick and glance around to make sure nobody else can hear us.

"Her mom found out we got married and got mad."

Daddy nods. "I understand that."

I sit back and let out a long puff of air.

"Nobody likes a surprise like that," he says.

"We both had a good reason for getting married."

"I hope it's because you love each other."

My throat tightens. I can only speak for myself on that.

"I've already told you I love her."

"Have you told her?"

I shrug. Too bad I didn't tell her before she flew across the world. Like a coward, I wrote her a letter and hid it in her purse.

"Well, does she love you?"

I shrug again.

"Son, do you know anything?"

"Just that she needed a green card to stay over here and get her job, and I needed a place to live."

Daddy leans forward. "A place to live? What's wrong with your trailer?"

I raise one brow. "It's condemned."

"Condemned?" His voice is loud enough for a few people near the barn to turn our way. He nods, then they go back to talking and eating their pork rinds.

"It was. I got a new one."

"You got a new place? Other than the one your mama and I bought?"

"I had to. The park is doing this updating thing where if your trailer is a certain age, they condemn it."

"Son, why didn't you tell me?"

I toss the stick in the fire. "I wanted to fix it myself."

"But it wasn't your fault. This isn't a bad grade or a

wrecked truck. You can't help what the neighborhood you live in does."

"I know, but you're always saying how I have to be a man now and take care of my own problems. I didn't want to disappoint you."

Daddy sighs and pops his knuckles. He's quiet for several minutes.

"It bothers me that you didn't think I'd help you," he finally says.

I shake my head. "No, Daddy. I knew you would help me, Mama too. And even Lacie and Collins, and anyone else here if I needed them." I span my arm across the yard to indicate all the family and friends milling around. "But I didn't want that. I wanted to take care of myself." I laugh. "Now that I think of it, marrying a girl with some money wasn't a solid plan for taking care of myself."

"If it makes you feel better, your mama likes to joke that if I die first, she'll remarry for money."

I frown. "Seriously, Daddy, I'm sorry."

He gives me a sympathetic stare.

"I know it was stupid not to come to y'all about the trailer."

"It was stupid, and it's stupid to marry for any reason besides love. But I am proud of you for taking responsibility."

"Thanks, that means a lot."

He rubs his chin and stares at the fire, then back at me. "So this whole time here y'all were pretending to like each other?"

"Honestly, I've had a crush on her for a while, but I always thought she was out of my league."

"Why's that?"

"She's the total package—pretty, smart, and mature."

"Son, plenty of girls like that would want to be with you if you start making mature decisions."

I shake my head. "What's strange is the most mature decision I made was agreeing to marry her."

"And now she loves you too?"

"I guess. I hope." I sigh loudly and pick up a new stick to poke at the fire. "We were pretty happy and liked each other —a lot—then she had to go."

"What happens when she gets back? Did you two have a plan?"

"To stay married at least a year to get her a green card and me graduated. But everything was going so well, I was certain we'd stay together. You know, like really be married."

"You need to talk to her." Daddy grabs my shoulder and gives it a shake before letting go.

"She texted me to say she got there safe."

He shakes his head.

"And I put a letter in her purse."

He shakes his head again. "Your generation doesn't understand the value of in-person communication."

"Daddy, she's halfway across the world right now. I'm not even sure what day it is there."

He holds up a hand. "I'm your father, and I know people. Let me help you like you should've let me with this stuff about the trailer."

I stab my stick in the ground and stare at him. "What do you mean?"

"You need to go to that island."

My eyes widen. There isn't a hint of humor in Daddy's eyes. He's seriously wanting to ship me off to talk to Carmelita. And I'm seriously going to let him.

# QUEEN OF MY DOUBLE-WIDE TRAILER

## *Carmelita*

Last night was not fun. Once I heard Antonio leave, I retreated downstairs for food. Between the time changes and jet lag, I couldn't remember the last time I'd eaten an actual meal.

Mama and Papa were waiting for me by the refrigerator like a pair of bloodhounds on the hunt. I guess I deserved that.

What I didn't deserve was to be told how I was rude to Antonio. Why does everything have to be about him? I marry another man, and they still talk about him.

They said it was a mistake letting me move to the States. Papa blamed himself, and Mama blamed me. Nobody blamed Antonio. He's the main reason I wanted to move.

You can't get away from him on this island. He's like David Hasselhoff in Germany.

I sat there and took my tongue lashing like a good daughter, then trudged to bed. It took me a while to fall asleep, and now I feel hungover.

I yawn into my bathroom mirror and pull my hair back in a ponytail. At least Papa made Mama agree not to bring up anything about Alabama or Liam again until after New Year's. However, she did promise to consult the family lawyer January 1.

The house is quiet, which I hope means my parents aren't home. They do a lot with the Parade of Pearls, which takes place in a few hours. I yawn again and slog down the staircase. The Christmas lights twinkle through the garland on the stair rail.

Mama's decorations are somewhere between Mrs. Sanderson's homey decor and her sister-in-law's flashy gold. They usually put me in the best mood, but not today.

During my lecture, I stared at the family tree behind my parents. But even my favorite ornaments couldn't combat the stress of my situation.

I go to the kitchen for some coffee and hear something in the next room. The housekeeper wouldn't be here the day after Christmas. My stomach buckles as I prepare to greet my mom. Maybe she's had time to cool down.

I tiptoe toward the sunroom and spot gray hair barely peeking above the back of a swing. My mood lifts when I get close enough to recognize Lola.

She smiles when I circle the swing and scoots until her short legs reach the ground. Before the swing stops for her to stand, I'm beside her, wrapping my arms around her neck.

Lola pats my back. "Baby girl, I've so missed you."

"I've missed you and Lolo most."

She pulls back and her eyes glisten. "Now that's not true. We've missed you most."

"I didn't expect you here."

She laughs. "Everyone else can work on that parade. I'm retired. I struck a deal with your mama to work on things here."

I follow her gaze to the table by the wall. It's covered with small gift bags.

"I finished it all in an hour, and my work is done." Lola smiles mischievously. She is the living definition of work smarter, not harder.

I lean back against the pillow behind me and swing us slightly.

"I'm glad you came home to see us."

I sigh. "I wanted to before, but I had some things pop up."

"Like a marriage?"

I frown and stare at my lap. "It's complicated, Lola."

"Try me."

I lift my head and stare at Mama's plants outside the glass wall. All the things that once relaxed me aren't working today. If it weren't for Lola's calming presence, I'd be a basket case.

"I married a friend to get a green card."

Lola clicks her tongue. "Honey, you know better than that."

"I know, but I want to stay in the States. It's different when you're no longer a student. I need new documentation."

"And that required marrying someone you don't love?"

I suck in a deep breath and exhale slowly. Lola stares at me, waiting patiently for a response.

"What's most complicated is I think I love him."

Her eyes widen.

"We've technically been married a few weeks and lived together a little less than that. This past week, we've kissed several times, and each time felt less like an act and more like we wanted it."

"And he feels the same?"

I nod.

Lola grins. "So what's the problem?"

"Other than my parents being mad, I guess nothing."

She fans a hand dismissively. "They'll get over it. They always do."

I twist my lips as last night flashes through my mind. "They're still hung up on Antonio. They sent him to pick me up in Manila and told me I was rude to him yesterday."

"His family are our closest friends. That's all."

I shake my head. "I don't think so. There's something deeper, like they're trying to force us together. I don't love him like that, and believe me, I've tried several times."

Her small hand rests on my knee. "I know you have, dear. And love shouldn't be forced."

"Liam offered to come with me here."

"Why didn't you bring him?" She perks up and smiles. "Jamil and I would love to meet him."

I smile. It's refreshing to know that at least my grandparents would be on board with what I want—and who I want.

"I didn't know how Mama and Papa would take it. The last thing I need is for them to interrogate him or take him to court or something."

"Dear, your parents want what's best for you. Have you tried explaining that Antonio isn't what's best for you?"

I stare at my feet and let Lola's wisdom soak in. I've married someone who isn't Antonio and started a job that wasn't with the family business. What I haven't done is communicate to my parents why.

"I'm guessing by your silence, you haven't."

I shake my head without looking up.

"Your parents love you as much as your lolo and I. They want you to be happy and raised you to be an intelligent young woman. You need to tell them that you're doing this because it makes you happy, not because you're rebelling."

I lift my head. "They think I'm doing this to rebel against them?"

Lola lifts her hands, then drops them in her lap. "I haven't heard them say that specifically, but I've read between the lines."

"I've never done anything out of spite. I just don't want to be with Antonio and live here forever." I turn to her and fight back tears. "You and Lolo are the main reason I come back as often as I do."

She pats my knee again. "Oh, dear. We so appreciate that, but don't let us hold you back from living your life where you want to live it."

I place my hand on hers and give it a quick squeeze.

"You know I wasn't happy when your mother first dated your father?"

"You weren't?" My jaw drops. Lola brags on Papa all the time and jokes that he is her favorite child.

"I didn't think he was good enough for your mother, as I'm sure your parents don't think anyone is good enough for you."

I huff. "Except Antonio."

"Even him."

I roll my eyes. "You should've been here last night."

"They know him and his family. He's a safe choice because they know what they're getting."

"But Liam is better for me in every way."

"Then you need to tell them that."

I sigh and rock slowly. Lola's right. Regardless of how things ended last night, I need to have another serious conversation with my parents. And the sooner, the better.

## CHAPTER EIGHTEEN

*Liam*

My family will either be really loved or really hated in a matter of minutes.

Popcorn popping and reclining chairs are the only noises as everyone settles in Uncle Earl's theater room. I'm in the back row, not all that concerned about the first episode of Aunt Carla's cookie show.

Mama, Carla, and G-Maw are anxious about our family looking like big rednecks on TV. Since I know we will—because how could we not—I'm more worried about my marriage.

The marriage I entered into as a business transaction written on a paper napkin. In the past few weeks, I've gone from wondering how we could make it last a year to wondering how I can make it last a lifetime.

Someone grabs my shoulder, and I turn to Daddy smiling. He rarely smiles, and when he does, it involves sports or guns.

"What is it?"

He stands and motions for me to follow him. Mama is waiting in the hallway with a suitcase. She hugs me and cries.

"Okay, did Pop or Nannie die? Because G-Paw and G-Maw are both in there."

Mama laughs and fans her face. "No, son. Ronald is here to take you to Carmelita."

"For real?"

She nods. I glance around, not seeing him.

"He's at Outdoorsmen Oasis. There wasn't enough space for the plane to take off from here since we have cows and goats in every pasture."

"I'll drop you off." Daddy smiles again, which is strange.

I follow him with my bag. Mama waves and wipes her eyes as we hurry down the porch. I fidget with my pocket knife to try and work out nervous energy. I almost call Carmelita, but decide against it.

In the note I left her, I told her to call me. The last text I got from her was that she made it home safely. I don't want to talk with her until she reads my note.

The only sign of life at Outdoorsmen Oasis is a plane parked in front of the store. I honestly don't see how we can take off from here any better than the pasture, but I trust Ronald.

He's a rich bachelor around my parents' age who spends all his spare time hunting, playing poker, and making corny jokes. I once thought he had the ideal life.

Except he isn't married.

I want to be married. It just took me marrying someone for the wrong reasons to make me realize I want her for all the right reasons.

"There's our Romeo." Ronald steps out of the shadows and smiles.

"Thanks for doing this," I say.

"No problem, boss. Your daddy was a big help getting the locals to support us building here."

I nod. They bought the land from Jack a few years ago for this store off the interstate. The land is in Apple Cart County, so the city and county had a lot to debate before it got built. I remember Daddy advocating for somewhere offering a decent number of jobs besides the mines. He always says the mines won't be there forever, which is one reason I planned on finding work in Tuscaloosa.

Right now, I only want to find my wife.

I grab my bag and swing it inside the plane soon as Ronald opens the door. Daddy waves and half smiles, which is more normal for his happy face.

I wave back and climb inside. Ronald hops in and slams the door. I scan the parking lot as he prepares to fly.

"Is this parking lot long enough to take off?"

"Nope."

My eyes widen. I buckle the seat belt and say a silent prayer. I choose to trust that if Ronald got it here, he can get it back. We roll toward the end of the parking lot, and I almost lose my lunch, dinner, and whatever else I've eaten the past week.

He hits the highway without a pause and flies down the interstate. An eighteen-wheeler heads our way and honks the horn. We ascend before getting too close and whoosh above it.

I'm glued to the seat, afraid if I move a muscle, we'll crash. Ronald laughs. I twist my neck to him watching me.

"You thought we were goners, huh?"

I nod.

"Boy, I've been flying longer than you were alive."

I wipe my brow and sigh. We're fully in the air, and I'm

still alive. Now I just need to make sure we're headed in the direction of Oval Island.

*Carmelita*

With all the lights downtown, it's hard to believe the sun has set.

Every storefront is decorated with rows of string lights and greenery. Lanterns hang on the streetlamps, and machines blow fake snow near the town square.

Since our island is so small, most people walk or drive golf carts to watch the parade. Then there's Lolo and Lola, who drive a moped. I love it when they put on helmets and climb on the tiny motor vehicle, Lola's arms around Lolo.

That's the kind of relationship I want to have. Not one that's all for show.

I'd thought my marriage with Liam was all for show until my feelings caught up with my actions.

I straighten my skirt and continue putting boxes of favor bags on our company's float. It's the same basic design every year—a huge oyster and pearl in the center. Mama mixes up the colors and smaller designs around it each year, trying to up her game from before.

This is the first year I can remember not helping decorate it.

"I need you to make sure we have enough to toss out at every stop," Mama says.

I slant my eyes toward Lola, who's beside me counting bags. She nods and winks.

"Uh, Mama, I need to talk to you and Papa before the parade."

"Now?" She taps her smartwatch.

"Yes, it's really important."

"I can line up the float, Diana. You two need to talk," Lola says.

Mama opens her mouth to say something, but Lola beats her to it. "Listen to your mother."

She clamps her mouth shut, and Lola smiles. "I'll take care of this like I did before you were old enough to care."

Mama forces a smile toward her mother and pulls me to the side, away from the parade floats. We stand in a shaded area between two of the downtown buildings.

"What is it, Carmelita?"

I cross my arms over my stomach as it hollows. "I love Liam."

She narrows her eyes. "The man you married without our permission."

"Mama, I'm twenty-four and out of college. I don't need your permission."

"Don't you think I know that?" The hurt in her voice stuns me. "It's hard enough to watch your only child move a world away—even harder when she talks about staying. Then when you hear she married an American, you know she's never coming back."

"Mama, that's not true. I'm here now."

She chokes. "Only because I threatened you."

"I wanted to come home for Christmas, but I was afraid."

"Of what?"

I kick the toe of my boot against the building and stare at the ground. "Of you and Papa pushing me and Antonio together."

"Why would we do that?"

I glare at her and sigh. "Because you always do, and

always have."

"I though you two liked each other."

"We do, did, whatever. I don't like him like that. I tried several times, but there's nothing there for me."

"And you love this Liam."

"Yes."

"Why were you in such a hurry to marry him? Couldn't we at least have met him first?"

I tighten my arms around my sides. "I needed to marry someone to stay in the States. I didn't know how to tell you and Papa I didn't want to move back and take over the company one day." My hands fly to my mouth.

Mama reaches out and cups my elbows. "Carmelita, why are you so afraid to tell us things?"

I shake my head and drop my hands. "I don't know. All my life I've done what the two of you have said. When you suggested school in America, I chose someplace far to see if I would really miss home. All I miss is the family. Not the business, and not Antonio."

She pulls me in for a hug. "Oh, baby. You need to tell us these things." Mama's watch beeps and she ignores it. "I don't want you to ever feel like you can't talk to us."

I hug her back. "Thank you."

Her watch beeps again.

"You better check that," I say.

She pulls her arm from around me and taps the screen. "We're close to lining up the floats. Marta says she wants you to ride up front on the town float and toss fake pearl jewelry to the kids."

I nod. "I'd be honored."

A smile creeps across my face as we head toward the floats. As a little girl, I admired the pretty lady up front tossing jewelry. I can't think of a better way to celebrate coming clean to my mom.

# CHAPTER NINETEEN

*Liam*

I just thought it would be better for Ronald to land in a pasture. We come to a rolling halt and take out what appears to be someone's rice crop. I clutch the dash of the plane and thank God I made it here in one piece.

A shorter man comes out of a small building, speaking a foreign language under his breath. He stands by the door to the plane and waits for us to exit.

"You missed the runway." His accent is heavy and his voice gruff.

"Sorry about that, boss." Ronald flashes a smile.

"You take out some of my crop."

"Again, we apologize." Ronald extends a hand. "Ronald Elmore."

The man shakes his hand. "Marino Martinez. I manage the airstrip, but this side is my crop too. Do you have a permit to park here?"

Ronald scratches his head. "I can buy one. Who do I pay?"

I shake my head. I'd have been better off taking a commercial flight.

Marino frowns. "No need to pay. I need permit."

Ronald presents a pilot's license that eases the tension a bit.

"Why you here?"

"I brought this young man to find his wife."

Marino looks at me for the first time and studies me.

"Do you know Carmelita Lim?" I ask.

His eyes go big. "You're the American!"

"Yes?" I cut my eyes to Ronald, then back to him.

Marino laughs. "The whole island talk about you."

"Do you know where I can find her?"

He nods. "Everyone is going to the Parade of Pearls."

My mouth twitches into a half smile. Carmelita's face lit up anytime she described the Parade of Pearls.

"Could you take us there?"

He nods again. "Get in truck."

We follow him to a tiny single-cab pickup. Of course, I get stuck in the middle. Marino shifts gears and almost castrates me in the process.

"Sorry," he mutters.

We turn down a small path between the crops and end out at a gravel road. Once we hit a paved one, I realize we left the plane and all my luggage beside a rice field in a foreign island. Ronald doesn't seem a bit concerned, sitting by the window making comments about palm trees and water.

A lot of the buildings are decorated for Christmas along the way. When we get to an actual town, everything is decorated, and if the crowd is any indication, we're the last three on this island to be downtown.

"Parade is about to start," Marino says.

He parks the truck at the end of a long line of golf carts. We barrel out like clowns at a rodeo. I stretch my legs before scanning the crowd for Carmelita.

The entire block is lined with decorated vehicles and golf carts. No animals or tractors though. The car across from us starts to move, and I crane my neck to find many more ahead of it driving away.

"Is she on a ride or in the crowd?"

Marino holds up a finger. He pulls out an old cell phone and expands a long antenna. Then he says something in his native language. After a pause, then a nod, he says one more thing, and hangs up the phone.

"Miss Carmelita is on the Queen of Pearls."

"What's that?"

"The front float. She toss out pearls to the kids."

"Okay?" I bounce on my toes, anxious to find her. When I start walking, someone grabs me.

"Slow down, guy. They come by here again." Marino nods as if he's a wise old man in a kids' movie.

I frown and turn to Ronald. He's chatting with two middle-aged women dressed like princesses. I puff out my cheeks and try to rein in my impatience.

Different vehicles pass us, along with dancers and bands in between. Despite the obvious cultural differences, this little island reminds me of a small town.

At last, there's a lag in floats and I hear drums behind us. People who weren't paying attention gather near the edge of the streets. I fall in place beside them and crane my neck.

Carmelita's face comes into focus. Her dark hair is covered with jewels, and she's throwing out more jewels. Kids cheer and people wave as she passes them, but I want to kiss her.

It takes all my self-restraint not to run back toward the float. A few minutes later, someone stands behind her and hands her more beads. It's a guy, and he's good looking and young.

"Who's that on the float with Carmelita?"

"Oh, that's Antonio," Marino answers casually, as if I'd asked for the time.

My nerves set on edge, heating my veins.

"Antonio?"

"Yeah, the governor's son. He—"

I don't stick around to hear the rest. That's all the clarification I need to know it's the one Antonio I don't want handing my wife jewelry.

*Carmelita*

I lift my hand to toss some necklaces, and feel them being tugged. I turn to Liam staring up at me, walking beside the float. He drops the ends of the necklaces and smiles.

My emotions flip between shock and satisfaction. The float stops, and so does the music. Liam hops over tissue paper and steps over pearls to get to me. I think I'm dreaming until Antonio speaks up from behind. "What's going on?"

Liam holds a hand up to him. "Excuse me. I have something to say, then I'll let y'all get on with this parade."

Antonio takes a step back and presses his lips tightly. Liam kneels beside me and takes my hand.

"Carmelita, I've been through a lot of pain since you left. Mentally and emotionally, obviously, and then I almost died twice in a plane."

"You did not," a man calls from the street.

Liam gives him a dirty look. "Now he decides to pay attention." He shakes his head at me. "Ignore him."

His face goes serious. "Nothing is right without you. In the short time we've been together, you have brought so much happiness to my life."

I swallow back a tear and focus on his blue eyes. Liam takes my other hand and sighs.

"I don't know your plans since coming back here. Maybe you want to stay now. I mean, your family lives here and the weather is nice. We married for reasons other than love, but somewhere along the way, I fell in love with you. I'd like to think you love me too. If not, that's fine. We can stay married for a year or call it quits now if you want to stay here. But for me, we're like the marriage line in the trailer. Without you beside me, everything will be off center and never really work right."

He drops my hand and fans his toward Antonio. "It's your choice. You can stay here and govern this island with the rich lawyer-pilot man who looks like the Asian version of a Ken doll, or you can come back to Alabama and be the queen of my double-wide trailer."

Before he can say another word, I lunge toward him and wrap my arms around his neck. He falls into my lap and kisses me.

We kiss like it's now or never, and in a way, it is. This is the defining moment where our relationship becomes real. Only when I hear cheers from the crowd do I realize we're putting on quite the show. I laugh into his mouth until he pulls back, laughing too.

"Does this mean you want to stay married?"

I nod, and Liam's smile covers his entire face.

"I had to ask. I was afraid you read my letter and decided not to call."

I wrinkle my forehead. "Letter?"

"Yeah, I put a letter in your purse before you boarded the plane. I explained my feelings in detail and said to call me if you felt the same way."

I squint, trying to recall if I noticed anything resembling a note in my purse. Maybe I mistook it for a grocery list or receipt?

"Here." Antonio pulls a folded piece of paper from his pocket and hands it to me.

My name is scrawled in Liam's messy handwriting. I run my finger across the writing, then give Antonio a questioning look.

"It fell from your purse when you jumped the gate. I took it to help you, then realized what it was and read it. I thought I was protecting you by keeping it, but you really do love him."

I give him a pitying look before turning to Liam. "I really do love him."

Liam cups his hand on my cheek and kisses me gently again. When he pulls back, his smile makes my heart melt.

"So what do you say? Will you come back to Auburn and help me govern the trailer park?"

I laugh. "Don't you mean modular home park?"

"I do."

"And I do too."

"I now pronounce you husband and wife," Antonio says.

We both give him a look. He smiles and shrugs. The chair I'm on shifts and we start to move. Everyone cheers again as the parade continues.

Liam sits beside me and looks panicked. "What do I need to do?"

"Throw stuff." I hand him beads.

He awkwardly tosses a necklace to the crowd. Antonio

hands more jewels to him. After taking them, he raises his hand for Antonio to shake.

A weight I didn't know I was carrying lifts when they shake hands and share a civil nod. We continue tossing jewels and waving to the crowd until we reach the parade's end.

Mama spots us and smiles. I'm not certain if she witnessed the scene when the parade paused, but I plan on catching her up.

"Come on." I grab Liam's hand and lead him off the float.

"Where are we going?"

I smirk. "To meet your in-laws."

# CHAPTER TWENTY

*Liam*

Carmelita jerks her head from my shoulder and pops her eyes open when the plane hits the pasture. She fell asleep on my arm hours ago, giving me plenty of time to talk Ronald into landing in the grass this time.

We come to a rocky stop a few feet from hitting one of Uncle Earl's cows. Still better than facing an eighteen-wheeler.

With all that's happened in the last few days, hitting a cow is the least of my worries. I didn't panic at all on the flight home, knowing that if I died, I'd do so with Carmelita by my side.

We spent last night on the island with her family. Seeing their fancy home, the expansive business, and the beauty of the island made me realize what all she gave up to be with me. Good thing I didn't see any of that before professing my love, or I might've chickened out.

Ronald cuts the engine and downs the last bit of his coffee. The Lims' housekeeper packed him several thermoses for the long flight. However, I'm sure he got more sleep than I did.

I stayed in one of the guest rooms. Even though everyone knows we're married, I didn't want our first real night as a married couple to be in her parents' house. We'll save that for the trailer.

Ronald opens the door and stretches. A few cows moo in the distance and one of Uncle Earl's security lights blinds us.

"Smile and wave for the camera, kids." Ronald shades his eyes with one hand and waves with the other.

"It's probably a motion sensor since he's expecting us," I say.

We unload the plane and stumble toward the edge of the pasture like we're staring at the sun. The gate opens when we come within a foot of it, proving Earl or Carla is watching for us. It closes once we're on the other side.

Between the pasture light and Christmas decorations, our path to the house is crystal clear. I notice my parents' SUV, as well as Lacie's van and more vehicles from my family. They must be gathering to eat more of the hog. Sometimes we have dinners between Christmas and New Year's with the fresh meat.

"Check this out." Ronald marches up and down the walkway, stopping at random to activate the music.

"Yep," I say dryly. I've experienced the synchronized lighting and music so much that I'm numb to it.

We climb the front porch, leaving Ronald to play with the decorations by the fountain. As soon as I ring the doorbell, the door swings open.

"Surprise!" Members of my family and other friends from town greet us in the hallway.

"What's this?" I direct the question to my parents, who are standing in front.

"A wedding shower. Carla planned it last minute, and we've been waiting on you two to get here."

Carmelita smiles widely, which makes me smile. Aunt Carla comes and hooks her arms through ours. She leads us to the living room, which is covered in white lights and white balloons, and sits us on a couch.

Lacie and Carly bring gifts by the armful and set them beside us as everyone gathers around.

Carmelita scans the presents near us, then everyone sitting around the room. Her eyes tear up.

"What's wrong?" I have a slight fear she might realize she's made a mistake not staying on Oval Island.

She shakes her head. "This is all too great. Thank you, everyone. I love Southern hospitality."

People laugh, cheer, and say, "You're welcome."

"Open your gifts," Aunt Carla encourages.

I gently rub Carmelita's upper back, then drag a heavy gift her way. We start with the first stack Lacie brought and work our way through a pile of everything from decorative women's stuff I'd never use to useful gifts like toilet paper.

"Now, you already have my gift. Remember?" Paul chews on a Rice Krispies bar.

"Yes, and thank you again," I say with a smile. How could I forget the mason jar wine goblets?

Carmelita glances around the room and sniffles. I hug her and kiss her cheek. She blots the corner of one eye, then smiles at the crowd. "Thank you all so very much."

Mama rushes over and hugs her. "We're delighted to have you in the family."

"There's plenty of refreshments in the kitchen," Carla says. She notices Paul licking his fingers and snarls. "At least there *was* plenty," she adds in a lower tone that only those of us closest to her can hear.

I laugh as I stand and pull Carmelita to her feet. "We're the guests of honor, which means they're all waiting on us before they can eat." I lean closer and whisper in her ear, "Except for Paul, of course."

She laughs and follows me to the kitchen. We fix plates of appetizers made from every part of a pig, along with wedding-themed cookies and sweet tea. In the center of the countertop is a wooden board covered with meats, cheeses, and bread.

"That board is another gift you can take with you," Carla says.

"Sanderson" is engraved at the top. I watch Carmelita's reaction when she reads it.

"You don't have to change your name," I offer.

The last thing I want is to pressure her into doing something she doesn't want. She's already given up so much to be with me. Besides, lots of smart, successful women keep their own names now.

She grins at me. "I want to share everything in my life with you, including my name. It's one of the first things I want to change when we get home."

*Home.* I sigh with contentment. No more jumping around dorms and extra bedrooms and childhood homes. Tonight we can officially arrive at our home—the double-wide trailer with a master suite. *Which reminds me. . .*

I wrap my arm around my wife and smile mischievously. "There is one thing I'd like to change before that."

She lifts her brows.

"I'd also like for us to share a room."

Carmelita blushes and stares at her plate. I grab a few more deer poppers, then lead her toward the back deck.

"Sounds like a good plan. Once we get to the trailer, you can cross the marriage line."

I give her a mischievous smirk. As luck would have it, there's mistletoe hanging above the back doorway. I pause and nod, lifting my eyes to the berries.

Her gaze follows mine, then settles on me. I pull her in for a quick kiss and stare into her dark eyes.

I can hardly wait to get the queen home to my double-wide trailer.

# EPILOGUE

*One Year Later*

*Carmelita*

"Honey, I'm home," Liam yells before opening the door fully.

I smile when he crosses the room and kisses my cheek. "Good day at work?"

"Yeah. Getting there." He pulls at the neck of his shirt.

I laugh. Every day, he can't wait to change out of his khakis and button-down shirt.

"I got the mail." He drops a stack of envelopes beside me on the couch.

On top is an official-looking letter addressed to me. I stare at the return address and my eyes widen. I hold it up and look at Liam.

He smiles. "I think so. Open it and see."

I rip open the top and pull out a paper. I unfold it and find a card with my photo. My green card. I smile and wave it toward Liam.

"Congratulations, you're officially a permanent resident."

I jump up and wrap my arms around his neck. He hugs me tightly.

"This has been the best year of my life, because of you," he says into my hair.

I exhale a long breath of contentment. "It's been the best year of my life, too."

We've seen a lot of change in the last thirteen months since we've gotten married. Liam graduated, we both started new jobs, and we moved—again.

"Come on, let's celebrate in my favorite spot." Liam leads me to the kitchen.

He grabs a jug of tea and the hideous jar goblets we got from Paul and Ms. Dot. He fills them and slides one my way. Then he opens the back door to the redwood deck he built when we moved the trailer this past summer.

We sit in the matching rocking chairs Liam snagged from the General Store on a trip to Wisteria. One of Paul's better finds from when he visited Amish friends in Tennessee.

Liam points to the open field in front of us. "One day, I'll build you a house on that hilltop."

I sip my tea and stare at the serene landscape. He found a good job in Tuscaloosa, and I was able to find a promotion there as well. We bought a few acres outside of town on the way to Apple Cart County, which made his family happy.

The last semester he was in school, he co-oped for the company and I started my new position. We quickly made a habit of sitting on the back deck and watching the sunset.

"Seriously, soon as we save enough, I'll draw out whatever house plans you want."

I rock in the slight breeze. "This may sound weird, and

I'm looking forward to a house, but I think I'll miss this place."

He cranes his neck toward the back door, then laughs at me. "The trailer?"

I shrug. "Well, yeah. We have a lot of good memories here. It's the first place that was ours together."

Liam stares at the center of the back wall and rubs his jaw, then grins at me.

"What if we keep the marriage line?"

I look at the piece of material joining the two sides of our double-wide.

"We can work it into a load-bearing wall or something."

"Or something?" I twist my face and study the trim.

"Like maybe hang it above the bed."

I roll my eyes. "I was going to suggest using it as a border for a flower bed."

Liam groans. "That would mean we have to plant flowers."

"I'll plant flowers."

"But then the dog will dig them up."

"We don't have a dog."

"Not yet." Liam raises one brow.

"You have a lot of plans, huh?"

He nods. "I do." He reaches over and takes my hand in his. "And I'm fine with whatever happens as long as it's with you."

I breathe deeply, and we lock eyes. Then he lifts his glass. "A toast to our future."

"To our future." I clank my glass against his and the jar separates from the stem.

I shriek as tea spills in front of us. Liam shakes his head. "At least we have a good excuse not to carry these ugly things into the future."

I tuck my feet under my legs before the stream of tea

reaches them. We both laugh as the sun sets in front of us. When it's almost below the pine trees at the edge of our property, Liam gives my hand a squeeze.

"No matter where we live, you'll always be the queen of my double-wide trailer."

## ACKNOWLEDGMENTS

First, I'd like to thank God for giving me creative ideas and placing the right people in my path to help see them to fruition.

My husband, Blake, gets credit next for always supporting my writing endeavors, even if he finds my stories a little too "girly and Hallmarkish." Of course, this book kind of broke the mold when it comes to that.

I also want to thank my readers and ARC team for their support. To all the people who read early, point out typos, post reviews, and cheer me on behind the scenes—You. Are. Awesome! I could not do what I do without my readers, and I love y'all!

Of course, I'd like to thank my editor, Joanne. She's always a pleasure to work with and polishes my books to help them shine. She also helped with some of the cultural references.

Speaking of cultural references, I want to thank my stepmom, Dyan, and dad, Roger, for answering questions about the Philippines and giving me some details that helped bring the fictitious Oval Island to life.

# TRY THE FIRST BOOK IN THE SERIES
## CHRISTMAS IN DIXIE

*Lacie*

"With a cold front moving in Christmas Eve, it looks like Atlanta might just get a white Christmas. So keep an eye on the roads. I'm Lacie Sanderson, on location in downtown Atlanta, wishing you all a safe holiday."

I put on the smile that helped me win Apple Sauce Queen my junior year of high school and wait for Dustin's signal. After an awkward minute, he nods, and the camera light stops blinking.

"That's a wrap, Lacie."

I immediately slump my shoulders and relax my quivering cheeks. "Thank God, it's freezing out here." That came out a little too southern, as does most everything I say when the camera isn't rolling.

"Well, you're headed west. Mark said the precipitation should fizzle out before it reaches Alabama."

I arch my eyebrow at Dustin. "No, it's going to move faster than Mark thinks. Alabama will have snow by Christmas morning, if not sooner."

Dustin shakes his head and chuckles. "Whatever you say, Lacie Bug."

I frown. He'll never let me live down the day my parents visited The Weather Channel and spilled the beans on my childhood nickname.

Dustin continues packing up his camera as I remove my earpiece. Once everything is put away in the news van, he wishes me a Merry Christmas and heads back toward the station.

I blow into my chapped hands and hop in my Honda CR-V. I turn on the heater and choose my favorite Christmas music station. It's only a few miles to my apartment, but it takes a half hour thanks to all the rush-hour traffic running both ways. I assume half the people are headed to work and the other half out of town. Over the past few years, I've met very few people in Atlanta who are actually from Atlanta.

After witnessing an exchange of horn honks and obscene gestures among my fellow commuters, I make it home. I've got to finish packing and make sure everything is in order so I can leave after seeing Collins. My insides warm, and I smile. Not the fake Apple Sauce Queen smile I reserve for on-camera, but my natural, not-so-over-the-top smile. Collins and I met on New Year's Eve last year and have dated ever since.

He checks off all my boxes. He's handsome, successful, smart, and compassionate, and he's been going to church with me. I can totally see us getting married one day. Which is why I've made every excuse under the sun to keep him away from my family.

As my G-Maw would say, they'd have him running like a chicken with his head cut off.

In high school, my daddy strategically cleaned his guns at the dining room table whenever a new guy would pick me up for a date. And he still says he can't understand why I broke up with Bradley. Ugh. From leading our high school football team to win state to serving as the Apple Cart County sheriff, Bradley Manning has made the whole town of Wisteria, Alabama, practically worship him.

I roll my eyes as I hop out of my crossover and lock the door behind me. Daddy is the least of my worries. My extended family is the real reason I want to keep Collins under wraps until I lock him down.

I go inside my apartment and take a whiff of the air. I should probably wash my egg skillet soiling in the sink before I leave. When you have to get to work before six a.m., you learn to let a few things slide.

I drop my purse on the tiny kitchen counter and roll up my coat sleeves. As I scrub the yellow scales on my not-so-nonstick skillet, my mind wanders. I imagine walking down the aisle toward Collins in a beautiful gown, with my arm looped through Daddy's. Then my perfect day is ruined by my crazy Aunt Misty whistling loudly and bringing everyone's attention to her improper choice of wedding attire.

I wince as I rinse the pan. Yeah, we're definitely eloping. With any luck, I can keep Collins away from the full Mayberry clan at least until the ink on our marriage license dries. Then it will be too late for him to cut and run, as G-Maw would say.

I reach for my hand towel that reads, "Christmas Cookies and Hallmark Movies." I dry my hands, then spread the towel across the counter and set the pan on top to dry. The hand towel takes up half my counter space.

When I moved to Atlanta, my choices were get a teeny tiny apartment or a roommate. And since I knew absolutely nobody and I'm not claustrophobic, I chose Option A. I'm not a huge fan of the city, but working for The Weather Channel has been my dream since fourth grade, when Jim Vann visited our school.

In Alabama, we have a weird hierarchy of celebrities. There's Nick Saban, the Alabama football coach, followed by two heavyset guys who have a radio show about little more than food and corny impersonations. Then there's Jim Vann. He's the king of weather in the southeast.

I've watched him navigate us through every storm throughout my life. I've always had a fascination with weather, but when he visited my elementary school and showed us weather graphs and polygons in real time, I made up my mind then and there to become a weather girl. But not just any weather girl. I wanted to anchor the news for The Weather Channel. And with an on-camera position in the field, I'm well on my way to fulfilling that dream.

I remove my coat and lay it across my purse, then head to my bedroom. My suitcase is already open on the bed, with most of my clothing folded beside it. I walk to my closet and stand on my toes to rummage through the top shelf. Or more like the only shelf. If I don't take my own coveralls, I'll end up wearing my brother's skanky hunting clothes to the family hog killing.

As soon as I smoosh my coveralls in the corner of my suitcase, I change out of my work clothes. The last thing I want to do is wear slacks, heels, and a blouse on a four-hour drive to the middle of nowhere, so I exchange that outfit for my thickest sweatshirt and some yoga pants.

I check my appearance in the full-length mirror hanging from my closet door. There. A bulky Mississippi State sweatshirt to make my brother mad, along with slightly faded elastic-waist pants. The perfect attire for Wisteria.

*Collins*

## TRY THE FIRST BOOK IN THE SERIES

My stomach churns as I get a text from Lacie saying she's done packing and ready for me to come over. I text back that I'm on my way and stare down at my own suitcase in the hallway.

She has no idea that I've managed to take off work and spend Christmas with her. I shrug on my jacket and slip out into the garage before my roommates ask any questions. They know I'm planning on visiting her family for the holidays, but they don't know my intentions.

I've known Charlie since rush week at Georgia, and he's sending vibes that he knows something is up. But I can't tell him or Mitch that I've had a diamond burning a hole in my pocket for several weeks now. Mitch would try and talk me out of marriage, as he's committed to nothing but noncommitment. And Charlie would act awkward around Lacie, since his weakness is keeping things on the DL.

I run a hand across my short beard and hop into my Land Rover. I feel a little silly dressed in scrubs, knowing I'm coming back here after leaving Lacie's. But she thinks I'm on call this weekend and that I'm going to the hospital after I leave her place. Lacie picks up on everything, which has made keeping secrets from her much harder than fooling the two goobers I live with.

We both live downtown, but I would like to buy a house in the suburbs once we marry. I know Lacie's only in Atlanta for work, and having a yard wider than my push mower might be a nice change of pace.

It doesn't take me long to get to her apartment building. I jump out and knock on the door. She answers right away and smiles up at me, her chocolate-brown eyes shining. I step inside and pull her in for a hug. She's warm and cozy and smells like flowers. I'm not sure what kind, but it's soothing. I've dozed off more than once on her couch while she snuggled up to me with her hair under my nose.

We both work crazy hours, but that's part of the commonality that kicked off our very first conversation. And her drive and ambition were a total turn-on from day one. Then her sweet-as-molasses voice sent me over the edge. It didn't take but a few months for me to know I wanted to marry that girl one day.

Lacie lifts her head and gives me a quick kiss before breaking the hug. I follow her a few steps to her tiny living room and take a seat on the couch. She plops down beside me. "Maybe you won't have to go in on Christmas Day," she says.

I shrug. With any luck, we'll be snuggled up at her parents' house celebrating our first Christmas engaged. "There's a good chance I will. I'm still the low man on the totem pole in surgery."

"Well, as someone who had to give a weather update at every fake Santa stationed in Atlanta last year, I can assure you working on Christmas isn't fun."

"But you had such a cheerful attitude doing it." I run my hand through her dark hair and smile.

"You didn't know me last Christmas."

"Not in person. But I still watched the weather." It was true. When I saw her at the hospital benefit on New Year's Eve, I knew right away she was the beautiful girl I'd watched deliver the weather every morning while getting ready for work.

Lacie leans back against my chest and sighs. "I'm gonna miss you this week."

"Yeah, and I'll miss you." I try to sound as if I'm not about to strike out toward Wisteria.

Lacie never says much about her hometown, except that it's small and she has a big family. It's probably one of those places with a gazebo downtown and Christmas wreaths on every streetlamp. Like in those low-budget Christmas movies I've suffered through the past month, all because I love her.

She raises her head and grins at me. "I better hit the road. The temperature is supposed to drop all day."

I chuckle and pull her close. "And you can't drive in the cold?"

She narrows her eyes at me. "No, it's gonna snow."

I laugh harder. "Okay, maybe here."

"No, in Alabama, too."

"Uh-huh." I nod my head.

She gives me the same face ornery patients do when I try and convince them that residents are real doctors. "Collins, I've been studying the weather patterns for Alabama all week. Trust me."

"Okay, babe." I raise my palms in surrender.

She stands slowly and reaches out her hand. I take it and stand in front of her, wrapping my arms around her small waist and pulling her in for a kiss. She fits perfectly between my arms, and all I can think about is how I can't wait to officially spend the rest of my life snuggled next to her.

After the kiss, I squeeze her in tighter, feeling her heart beat against my chest. It's all I can stand to not go ahead and propose right here, in her living room, while she's dressed in sweats and I'm in my scrubs.

But Lacie deserves better than that. She's old-fashioned and high-class. I need to meet her parents before I propose and let them know my intentions. Then I need to plan the perfect proposal. Someplace outside. Heck, maybe even in a gazebo. Someplace special, where she'll always remember that moment.

After a long minute, I pull away, knowing she's anxious to get on the road. "I'll put your bags in for you."

"Thanks."

I follow her to the door, where she has way too many

bags for a few nights. But she always overpacks. I've never understood that. I could go to the moon with only one suitcase.

I take her two biggest bags, and she follows me with a fancy duffle and her purse. I maneuver them all to fit best in the back of her crossover and close the hatch. She smiles and kisses me gently on the lips.

I smile back. "Merry Christmas, Lacie."

"I'll be sure to call you when I get there. Wisteria doesn't have the best cell service, so I'll call from Mama's. You'll have the house number that way, too."

I nod. "I love you."

"I love you, too." Her eyes sparkle as those words leave her pink lips. My heart skips a beat, and it takes everything in me to not jump in her vehicle and suggest we elope.

Instead, I run my hand down her hair and squeeze her cheek. Then I go to my own vehicle and drive back home. By now, my roommates are on their way to work, so I can get packed and head toward Wisteria.

My hand trembles as I fumble with fitting my key into the garage door. I'm going to a place I've only heard about, with no real plan of how or exactly when I'll propose. I'm thinking Christmas Eve, but the lack of certainty behind it all makes my mouth go dry. It's not like me to not have a plan.

I go inside and change out of my scrubs and into khaki pants and a buttoned shirt. My usual look outside of work. Then I get to packing.

After stacking my clothes and tossing in my toiletries bag, I fumble around the bottom of my sock drawer. There. I bring out the tiny black box and pop it open. The corners of my mouth raise as I admire my grandmother's diamond. As the only child and grandchild, she left it to me for my future

## TRY THE FIRST BOOK IN THE SERIES

bride. I've already had it sized to fit Lacie, thanks to sneaking one of her rings to the jeweler's.

I close the lid and exhale a huge breath. Then I tuck the box securely in the inside zipper pocket of my suitcase. I take a quick glance around my room to make sure I didn't miss anything, then head outside.

As I climb into the driver's seat, a knot forms in my stomach. I'm about to drive hours away to a town I have no idea about to meet people I've only seen in photos, then propose to the woman I love. But if it ends with Lacie promising to be my wife, it will all be more than worth it.

# ABOUT THE AUTHOR

Kaci Lane is a journalist turned fiction writer who believes all stories should have a happy ending. While unsuccessfully trying to learn Spanish for a decade, she has become fluent in sarcasm, Southern belle and movie quotes. She is married to a Southern Gentleman and has two young children who help keep her humility in check. Connect with her on kacilane.com or Facebook.

## BOOKS BY KACI LANE

**Bama Boys Series***

*Hunting for Love*

*Chicken about Love*

*Hammered by Love*

*Cutting out Love*

*Geared for Love*

**Apple Cart County Christmas**

*Christmas in Dixie*

*Crazy Rich Rednecks*

*Queen of my Double-Wide Trailer*

**Schooled on Love Series**

*Taco Truck Takedown*

*Side Hustle*

*Buggy List*

*Off-Season*

**Books in Shared Series with Other Authors**

*No Time for Traditions*

*A Perfect Match in Silver Leaf Falls*

*If you enjoyed the Apple Cart County Christmas books, revisit Apple Cart County with the Bama Boys series, starting with *Hunting for Love*. Set in Apple Cart, Alabama, it includes secondary characters from the Christmas series.

www.ingramcontent.com/pod-product-compliance
Lightning Source LLC
LaVergne TN
LVHW041800060526
838201LV00046B/1063